The light is for the heroes, and when they left, the real light went with them. We are now creatures of the darkness and the shadows, whether we know it or not. There were creatures in that darkness when we left it, and we have forgotten them, but now we rediscover the real perils. . . .

M.A. FOSTER
has also written:

THE WARRIORS OF DAWN

THE GAMEPLAYERS OF ZAN

THE DAY OF THE KLESH

WAVES

THE MORPHODITE

TRANSFORMER

OWL TIME

A Collection of Fictions

M. A. FOSTER

DAW BOOKS, INC.
DONALD A. WOLLHEIM, PUBLISHER

1633 Broadway, New York, NY 10019

DAW Collectors' Book No. 612

First Printing, January 1985

1 2 3 4 5 6 7 8 9

PRINTED IN U.S.A.

CONTENTS

This book is dedicated with affection respect and regard to

SAM McCLURE, Springfield, Oregon

PREFACE

This book is several things, but first let me say that it isn't: it isn't an anthology of reprinted material from the magazines—any magazine, fair or foul, pro or fanzine, pulp or slick, small-press or large.

It is four short novels, three of which were written especially for this publication. The one exception which does have a prior history is included here because the writing of that story and one other—not included here— inspired the idea to try this. This is a package, a concept album, and an experiment in publishing.

This month, I have been writing professionally for ten years. During that time I have observed the closing down of four SF magazines with which, in a very large sense, I grew up. Similarly, in that same time, I have seen half a dozen more new magazines arise—and also go down in their turn. It is not pessimism and negative attitudes to conclude from this that the market for short fiction has dramatically shrunk: it is simple and practical realism.

There are other observable facts and trends which align with this. Here is not the place to list them, nor is it the place to leap up on a stump and, with zeal and true-believerhood, denounce villains, assign causes, lay blames. That is not my intent, in the stories or in this introduction. But this may be such a place and time to attempt something different, and admittedly commercially risky.

It is legitimate to ask why, after six novels which have done reasonably well, would I attempt "four short novels under one cover"? After writing two on assignment for George R. R. Martin in the *New Voices* series, I discovered, to my amazement and dismay, that what I actually knew about writing was only a tenth of what I thought I did. More importantly, short fiction is the place where the writer learns brevity, discipline and control—and where the reader has come to be astounded, amused, outraged, entertained, and have-mind-blown-away. And somehow I had made a ten-year run in SF without working that short fiction territory, except for the *New Voices* project, and this. As soon as I tried it, I understood what I'd missed. And maybe what my readers missed as well.

Up front, then: each of these stories included here is an exercise in using my plots, themes, notions and characters in styled settings which intentionally suggest the manner of older writers whom I have admired along the way. The process is much like learning music—you have to learn the licks and runs of others before you can learn to make your own unique sounds.

The Man Who Loved Owls is intended to suggest J. G. Ballard.

Leanne is after the manner of Ray Bradbury— or Harlan. Take your pick.

The Conversation is intended to reflect a mix of Jorge Borges, Vladimir Nabokov, and Franz Kafka.

Entertainment follows the excellent example of Jack Vance.

These are my dues, which have been long in coming. If this works for you as it did for me, then perhaps someday we'll try it again. If you have gotten this far, thanks. We need good writers in SF—but we also need good readers, too.

—M.A. FOSTER

THE MAN WHO LOVED OWLS

This one started out as a title which sounded as if
it had interesting possibilities. It turned out to have
surprising depths and alarming undercurrents, and
proved to be most difficult. I can offer only two
hints: the man who loved the owls turned out to be a
minor character, and the tale, in a classic bit of
misdirection, isn't about music at all.

For George R. R. Martin, because you asked.

> "*And the stars we could reach
> Were just starfish on the beach.*
>
> —*Seasons in the Sun*, (McKuen-Brel)

Palmyra Sound, Coquina Pass, Turquoise Island Beach
and all its string of indistinguishable beach towns:
Pack's Landing, Tusuque, Trocadera, Cayo Ameca,
Cochicabamba, Rivadavía, Flor de Luna, Cerro Gordo,
Arrirang, Torre Quemado, Mutiny Point, Cabo de

Las Perdidas. The future is here, but the beach goes on forever, the names changing but not the realities underlying the names. Or the unrealities.

Opening night in Pack's Landing, at Lillie Mae's Reliable Mingo Club, for Twilight's Last Gleaming, which is us: Rommy, Pablo, Suzanne, Kim and me, Sain. Lillie Mae's is an old barrackslike building with all the first-floor inside partitions knocked out, and the walls on three sides are salt-grayed wooden louvers. The bar and the bandstand take up the fourth wall. The lighting is poor, and the sole decorations are multicolored graffiti, applied by hands, brush, spraycan. Behind the stage, high up, someone had once painted:

TO DO IS TO BE—SARTRE.

Below this, someone had added later, in a different color and style:

TO BE IS TO DO—KIERKEGAARD.

But at the bottom, a third savant had summed up the final significance, in a heavyhanded lettering that combined germanic *fraktur* and L.A. Chicano:

DO BE DO BE DO—SINATRA.

To the left, red lettering asserted: UNDER CAPITALISM, MAN EXPLOITS MAN. UNDER COMMUNISM IT'S JUST VICE-VERSA. To the right, a meticulous hand had inscribed: A CONSERVATIONIST BUILT HIS BEACH HOUSE LAST YEAR. A DEVELOPER WANTS TO BUILD HIS NEXT YEAR.

We play a mix of our own stuff and old beach favorites so old that they were moldy-oldies in our parents' days. Some dance, others lean back on the louvers and listen, some drink, and some leer and hustle. We slide into our windup number, "Coffee," with its heavy old-time blues feel and classic progression C6-C7-F7-C6-G7-C6, and a few of the patrons perk up a bit and smile in the choruses, which end with the song's crude credo:

"*They call me 'coffee' 'cos I grind so fine.*"

Toward the end, a few were even singing along on the choruses. In another hour the eastern sky will start coloring, up the beach somewhere beyond Cayo Ameca.

The lights fade and in the post-set daze we start tearing down; we don't have roadies. Suzanne puts her guitar away as if it were a baby being tucked in for the night. Kim stares at her percussion kit as if she didn't know what it was for. Pablo holds his acoustic guitar by the neck like a sack of potatoes and scans the crowd, looking for the face with a certain light in her eyes. Rommy shuts down his keyboards in an unvarying sequence, ignoring everybody, closing lids and fastening snaps.

I put my bass up, unplugging, and locking its case, and like Pablo, scanning the crowd. Farther off, across the smoky room, fragrant with hemp like autumn leaves, a group has been lounging by the bar. I couldn't see them with the stage lights on, but now I can. They look different, an odd group. I poke Rommy and point with my head, and he glances that way. He is our mobile beach gossip file. He knows everybody.

"I see 'em."

I ask, "Know them? The ones not wearing bikini bottoms."

He looks upward, as for divine guidance, and begins, "The guy in the white suit is Miles Penderecky, the architect. The one in the steelrim specs and crewcut is the composer Boris Deligny. The broad in the white slinkdress with the ass-slit is Merilu Tololo, actress, model and occasional mistress, now Penderecky's. I don't know the unisex unknown in the OD overalls. The other guy is Holden Czepelewski. The dark woman with the swanlike neck is Yiva Dandim, the famous Israeli opera singer."

"Czepelewski, you say? Not the mad poet?"

"The same, none other, one each, non-flying." Rom looked at me, significantly, lowering his head so he glared out from under his neolithic eyebrows. "Don't get involved with those people."

"Why?" I always ask why.

"Never mind why. Just don't. That's all you need to know."

I had heard of them all at one time or another. Penderecky was famous for his strange and dramatic public spaces, always for ostensible uses, but all with the odd air of stages for intricate and involuted emotional dramas: concrete in fourteen shades of White and Sand. His mall over on the mainland, "A Whiter Shade of Pale," had already been the scene of several crimes of passion, holdups, and hostage-takings.

Deligny was equally notorious, his neoclassical music demanding upon listener and performer alike, combining the dissonances of Orff and Hindemith within the time structures of John Cage, exemplifying the worst excesses of Musique-Concrete. He had been known more than once to conduct wearing a hardhat, when leading one of his pieces, "Symphonie-Pneumatique", with its braying choruses of tuned air horns taken from ruined trucks and locomotives.

Czepelewski had been the mad and moonly poet of a former generation, extolling chaos, disorder, violence, anarchy, malice, vandalism and bad attitudes, through his works *Death the Bride* and *Hour of the Assassins* (essays, so to speak), and his anthologies of poetry *I Gave You Diamonds You Gave Me Disease*, *Prisoner of Her Own Device*, *The Master of the Cesium Mine*, and *The Lips I Have Kissed Were Not All on Faces*. He had rejected fame as he had rejected order, and now associated with Penderecky as foreman, arranger of deals, factotum and overseer. He was rumored to be wealthy from the exploitation of loathsome vices and rapacious habits, but perhaps that was only the spirit of the Age, Envy, speaking, as they denounced the thing they secretly wanted. And perhaps Czepelewski had only been lucky and clever, certainly a matter of good timing but not impossible.

He did not appear to be an exemplar of evil, but wore a dark, loose shirt, open at the neck, and loose pants of similar coloration, simple and direct. The effect was that of a medic's uniform, or perhaps an obscure laborer off on a holiday, scowling at the salt on the rim of his Margarita, and occasionally leering at the overly earnest hustlers who spent their evenings at places like Lillie Mae's. There was, however, one way he differed from his companions. *They* were slumming, poseurs one and all; but whatever Czepelewski really was, it was no pose, but deadly serious and totally within the here and now. I looked away for a moment at the crowd, and when I looked back, he was gone, although the others were still there.

Behind Lillie Mae's is one of the old beach houses, where they put up the bands. Quiet and dark now. And Kim is waiting in the deep shadows under the latticework, among the oleanders, her pale face and enormous dark eyes the only things I can see with certainty. Then she steps away from the house, all the nerves and distraction gone, now become herself, an orphan, a waif, a tired, skinny, fragile girl, unfocused with first-night blues, reaching.

"Where do you think you're going?" Kim has a permanent whine in her voice, a brattiness, that takes getting used to. And on other occasions, a throaty insistent husky murmur that hints of the unspeakable dreams.

"Walking."

"Yeh, you say. You always walk afterwards, go look at things you shouldn't. Get into trouble." She always talked that way, as if there were a bad connection between the inside of her and the outside. But I had grown to like it; sometimes it was pure poetry, and when we left her alone she could write beautiful, surrealistic, haunting lyrics no one could properly understand. They aren't supposed to.

"Come on, let's go get into trouble together. Strange brew, something inside of you."

"No. Sleep. You hold me. That's good."

"You always complain that I'm too hot."

She opens her arms and leans into me, her hair a mass of frothy curls, her body soft, slender, ribs and bones. I smell the sweat in her hair, a tart, clean, salty scent. Her skin is cool and damp. I say, softly, "Come with me, listen to the ocean. We'll find a dune, and listen, and wait for the sun."

White teeth flash in the dark. "Naked people don't feel mosquitoes."

We cross the now silent and empty beach drive, leaving the dark hulk of Lillie Mae's behind us, cutting across by the Zoo Baba, a venue for abrasive, nihilist bands with their messages from Interzone of doom and hopelessness. The street, the houses, the amusement park—all empty, abandoned, dark. Then a patch of sand, sea-oats, dark patches of Yaupon-holly, and then the open secret emptiness of the nighted ocean. The tide is high, but there is no wind, and what little surf there is, is sullen and abrupt, striking the shore in dull, petulent little slaps and hollow dull thuds, flat and timbreless. To the west is a string of colored lights, over the water, reflecting. Kim whispers, half-singing, "I see the lights, I see the party lights, they're red and blue, and green. . . ." I feel her narrow hips brush mine as we walk, and I say, to fill the void, "Pack's Landing Pier," like some tour guide.

For a long time we say nothing, drinking the ocean, the listless flaccid surf, the pier lights, the stars, the stars we know that we will never have. Scorpio fills

the oceanside sky, clearing the horizon out over the
heaving black waters, immense, significant. Antares,
Dschubba, Graffias, Zuban Al Akrab, Shaula, Jabbah,
Alniyat, Lesath, the beautiful Arabic ringing names
of the stars, the smooth curve across the dark sky. A
long time. Once Kim and I had looked into each
other's eyes and the summer sky and lived through a
brightly piercing time of fascination and desire, truly
we had traveled to the end of the rainbow, reaching
through eroticism for a brighter core of each other
that we never touched, only glimpsed. I awoke mornings with the seashell taste of her body still on my
face. Now faded, muddied, but never really ended,
either. We forgave everything: that's the measure of
it.

We find a dune, somehow catching a scrap of
seabreeze, and settle down, sinking now into fatigue.
I cradle her to me and kiss the thin mouth, and she
returns it, sleepily, letting her tongue linger on the
inside of my upper lip, a slick, hot little muscle, but
there is no fire in it, and she settles, relaxing, secure
at last in the crook of my arm, fading into sleep even
as she adjusts her body into the last position; a door
being closed. Not slammed. Just closed.

In the sky, still dark, over toward the east, the
satellite glides out of the north, moving south, out
over the ocean, picking up the light of tomorrow, not
just a bright speck moving, but visibly a round wheel
with five spokes, rotating. Not L-5, but E-1, or so
they call it officially. The people call it The Eye in
the Sky, or Wheel of Fire, or sometimes, Proud

Mary. Five years it's been up there, mostly reminding us of what we'll never see or have.

E-1 drifts off into the southeast, still flashing silver fire, and the sky stays dark. After a measureless time I see something odd down the beach toward the pier. I'm not aware of when I notice it. It's just there: off in the indistinct distance there's a shape moving, a person, walking oddly, or perhaps dancing, and darker shadows move and weave around it. I can't tell if it's man or woman, but it moves easily, silently, flowing to the rhythms of an unheard music I couldn't guess at. But whatever it is, there's something of the nightmare to the motions, an undefinable sense of cruel and pitiless menace; like music, dance can be very beautiful and at the same time oppressively threatening, although if pressed, one could not say precisely what the threat exactly was. But as it moves, in its motions, it is aware, it interacts with the night world around it. It knows the stars, the surf, the lights along the pier. And it knows Sain and Kim, hidden though we are in the hollow of a dune.

A soft, indistinct sound grows out of the background of the wind, almost not moving, and the water, heaving and tossing; a burry, blurred muttering, and down there, an indistinct shape looming behind the moving figure and the shadows. It throws up its arms in a histrionic gesture of finality, and the fleeting, darting shadows wheel and vanish. I rub my eyes, and look again, and there is only the larger object, growing smaller, its noise fading to inaudibility. I know that noise, but I can't remember it. It moves

off down the beach and vanishes, at exactly the
moment I look back to the east and see pale blue
light of predawn beginning to give shape to the glassy
waves. I feel a puff of air behind me, and sense
something out of the corner of my eye, large and
dark, soft and effortless, but it's gone before I can
find it. I shiver, not from dawn cold. Kim pulls
herself closer to me and mutters something in the
incomprehensible speech of sleepers; but pleased with
it, for a faint smile flickers at the corners of her
mouth.

Pablo has a soft, babyish face, olive, lustrous skin,
and an indulgent softness about the middle. In five
years it will graduate to a full-fledged paunch. Aside
from the fact that he plays acoustic guitar to make the
angels hang their heads in envy, he always seemed to
be a harmless species of nerd. But for reasons
inexplicable, women find him irresistible, while Rom
and I chase after them madly—and usually without
result. Never mind. Our gifts and our curses alike are
random.

Coming out of the shower into the golden, slanted
afternoon sunlight, I see two figures out on the railed
porch facing Lillie Mae's, Pablo and one of his
pickups, now all smiles and private conversations.
This one is embarrassingly plain about the face, square-
jawed like a boy, almost homely, but she has a long,
lean, graceful body so beautiful you almost can't
stand to look at it, gleaming with a sheen of oil,
tanned to a lovely sand-brown color, and wearing a
bikini so small that its material wouldn't have filled

the top of an Aspirin bottle. It conceals, in fact, nothing, nor is it intended to.

Inside, Kim lies in an enormous towel on the sofa, naked and moon-pale, half-wrapped in the striped expanses. I can smell soap. Now she looks particularly fragile and exotic, with her exploding-curl hair, jet black, and her pale, thin body. We always told her that if she couldn't go on as a musician she could always pose for reprints of the cover jacket of *I Escaped Hitler's Ovens*.

I say, "Why aren't you outside?"

"Can't handle the heat. It spoils my moon-tan. Have to leave the tans to Suzanne, or to that tart Pablo picked up last night."

"What's her name?"

"Barbara." Kim rolls her eyes and says it again, now drawing it out: "Bah-Bah-Rah." And then again, as an afterthought, "Bahbah. Nee Nee Na Na Nu Nu."

I mutter, "I'm in love, take me downtown."

She stretches and says, after a moment, "I had bad dreams last night."

"Sleeping with me. I'm too rich for your blood."

"We didn't *do* anything. At least nothing memorable."

"Aha! We should have! Then you would have . . . ."

She shakes her head. "Nonononono. You I remember. Always good. I had dreams about owls, and an evil sorcerer who commanded them, who. . . . I can't remember."

"The Crewel Owel!"

She giggles, and then a darker shadow crosses her

face, like a bad memory. "Distorted, but very clear, very real. *I saw it*. But I couldn't say what it meant. I keep thinking of those Hindu religious paintings, but not that exactly. That style, but gods like Egypt, you know; human bodies, but heads of animals and birds. . . ."

"There's a song coming. I can tell." I sing, falsetto-blues:

> *'There we laid all sweaty in the bed,*
> *Angels and devils runnin' through my head.*
> *I don't mind you callin' me another man's name,*
> *But when you call me 'Tyrone' was a cryin' shame.'*

Kim shakes her head, groaning over the corny lines. "I won't write anything like that. No songs about this at all."

"You know, Kim, we could make an album of your nightmares."

"Hah. What would we call it?"

"*Dentes Frendentes Video:* I See the Gnashing Teeth."

At 10:30, the bartender wipes his hands on a bar-rag, steps up, and introduces us, while we stand behind him, looking only as dumb as musicians can while waiting for their cue. "Twilight's Last Gleaming," with our modest poverty albums "Street of Dreams, "Rainbow Rider," and "No Turn Unstoned."

Tonight we open with Rommy, at first solo, doing the first bars of Bach's Toccata in D Minor, with that creepy air that makes one think of Boris Karloff laboring over an Art Deco organ, demented. But then

Kim and I come in together, with an insistent, driving 4/4 pound that runs the pace up and keeps it up until the end. That always gets their attention. Then we go into a couple of our "dirty" numbers, "L'il Fat Chicken Muscle" and "So-So," with its suggestive chorus,

" *'So so' you couldn't touch it wif a powder puff!*"

Suzanne and Kim trade vocals on their specialty song of two girls with the same lover, "Focus-Bofus, Hocus-Pocus," and after that the crowd is ready to listen.

We switch leads to me, and over a light, feathery bass line, simple syncopated walking, I do "Guilty as Charged":

> *It isn't that you done me wrong,*
> *It's just I like to blame you.*
> *It isn't you're a bad girl,*
> *It's just I like to shame you.*

> *I'd like to make you happy for a while—*
> *Feel good; I'd like to love you for a*
> *little—*
> *If I could.*
> *But I gotta get out*
> *Before I get got-out on.*

After a short pause, Kim puts on her headset mike, which makes her look like a manic telephone operator; she takes lead on her own song, "Yojimbo," singing in her most piercing, most bratty voice. Amplified, she really has a voice that could worm a dog.

"Psychopath savior gonna break down the walls,
    And lead us to the garden of paradise."

And when the music dies away for the last line of "Yojimbo," she goes up on her very highest cymbal, a tiny ziljian, and whispers,

"So under the spreading chestnut tree,
    I sold him and he . . . sold me."

I look up, half-blinded by the lights, and among the wild audience I think I see Czepelewski and friends by the bar. They are smiling, clearly having a good time, and Czepelewski raises his Margarita in a salute of glittering intensity.

We take a break, to get our wind back. I take a sweaty beer glass from somebody and turn it up. And recognize the creature in overalls from last night. Right in front of me, and I still can't tell quite what it is, male, female, or something otherwise. But it says, in an unmistakable female voice, although deep, "The Captain wants to know if you know 'The Bold Marauder.' "

I feel the beer, the heat, the running river of excitement of the crowd—an organism stirring—and nod. She produces another cold beer from behind her and says, "The Captain says, then do your best."

I down the beer and call to Pablo, "Bold Marauder." He nods over the noise, catches Suzanne's attention, and we front three fall into it, opening deliberately clumsily, letting Kim and Rommy catch on, fall in and tighten it up. It starts out like a folk protest song, sarcastic, but as we go, we tighten it up until it becomes an anthem of violence. Suzanne and Kim double on the choruses, screaming in unison like demonic cheerleaders:

> *"O it's heigh, ho, hey—I am the bold marauder!*
> *Heigh, ho, hey—I am the white destroyer!"*

I looked for Czepelewski; he had requested it. He was totally entranced, and on the last chorus, raised his glass in another salute.

After the set, locking up our instruments, the creature in overalls joins us, and says, quietly, "The Captain offers his hospitality; come up and visit. Enjoy."

Suzanne says, glowering under her eyebrows, "All of us?"

"Whoever's a mind to. No problem. I have wheels." Sensing an argument, or at least dissension, she sidles off, out the door into the predawn darkness, dense with night-creatures singing in a deafening hum.

Suzanne says, slowly, "I don't like that guy or any of his friends. He's a creep, so are they. A degenerate!"

I say, facetiously, "You mean 'decadent,' don't you?"

She turns down the corners of her pouty mouth a little more, a sure sign of trouble, and says, "Those people are way over our heads. I won't go. Wrong."

Pablo agrees with her, although we all know his reasoning and his agreement to be more than transparent: tall Barbara with the square-jawed plain face had been in the audience. But the rest of us want to go, at least to see if we can gather a little influence for a better booking, say, at Rivadavia, or even Flor de Luna. In the end, Pablo and Suzanne leave. The rest of us leave through the back door into the night, trying to look as unaffected as possible. As usual, Kim has no difficulty looking totally distracted.

Outside, by a corner of the building, they are waiting for us, Czepelewski, Tololo, and the girl in overalls, who we learn is called Karen. In the dark, she seemed less homely, and now wore her overalls open to the navel, and seemed to glow with an inner light, an animation that made her interesting and magnetic. Beauty, after all, is only an expression of a social function, while desire is a projection of the deepest self.

Kim, oddly, responds to Czepelewski, babbling, while Rommy, for all his cynicism, basks lazily in the warm glow of the slightly-past-prime Tololo.

Of middle height and easy in his movements, Czepelewski is graying and thin on top of his head, balding, but apparently in excellent shape, with a trim midsection and powerful shoulders. But there is a contradiction in him that makes me uneasy: his accents and patterns of speech are indeed those of a laborer, a roadmender out on the town, but the content of his remarks carries the shadows of an immense worldliness and sophistication. He pronounces the word "cement" as if it were spelled s-e-a-m-i-n-t.

We turn the corner to the empty lot to board his vehicle, which is marvelous and strange, even for the beach. Merilu explains in her throaty voice that once it had been a mobile crane, used to erect the enormous advertising signs that used to punctuate the landscape. But when the signs were outlawed, cranes were surplus, and Penderecky had gotten it for a song. For a time, they had used it to erect concrete pylons bearing wind chimes made from old compressed-gas cylinders, which made mellow booming tones audible for miles. But then Czepelewski, who was handy with welding torch and arc-cutting electrode, one day torched the whole crane body and turning table off the frame, retaining only the old pulley sheave and the hook for objets d'art, mounted them on bone-white concrete pedestals before his rambling house in Cochicabamba, afterward admiring with the cultivated taste of the true connoisseur the rust that soon streaked the concrete.

The remainder he converted into a mobile party platform which he would take out on the beach from time to time. The cab was unchanged, more or less, although he reworked the interior extensively; the hydraulic outriggers he retained as well. But aft of the cab, he built on the deck of a yacht, with teak railings, brass fittings (which Karen solemnly polished) and genuine Kauri Pine decking. Overhead, in place of the sail, billowed a striped canopy bordered with tassels and fringes, for which reason he called it "The Furry with a Syringe on Top," a very moldy play on words. However whimsical its name, it was powered by a diesel engine from the old days which whined and roared in a satisfactory manner, able to vent its exhausts out through a set of splayed organ pipes which resonated in strange dissonances. It could also run silently.

Czepelewski climbs up, while Karen disappears
into the dark cab, and waves us aboard with a lordly
gesture, and then rapping on the cab roof, and without a lurch, the Furry majestically and silently trun-
dles off into the night. The ride goes against all
expectations, smooth and firm. Karen lets the machine roll effortlessly, gliding along the beach road
until she finds an access out to the sand, and turns
onto it, sluffing through the soft sand on its ten
wheels until it feels the hardpack of the beach proper
underfoot. Czepelewski produces a magnum of champagne from a cooler, produces glasses, and shouts
into an antique speaking-tube, "Full speed ahead and
damn the torpedoes!" And somewhere far away I
hear, or feel, Karen working up through complicated
gears, and then there is wind, then a strong wind,
and then very strong, gale force. Small craft warning.
Karen turns on the exhaust organ, Czepelewski turns
on floodlights, and we, ignoring the wind, settle into
deepsea fishing chairs to enjoy the ride to Cochicabamba, drinking like desert nomads. Karen takes him
at his words and lets the heavy machine have its
head, and so sometimes on hard sand, and sometimes
in the edge of the surf, we fly west, the humid wind
whipping our hair; and the exhaust organ builds up
into a stunning powerchord in a minor key. Dorian
Mode, I think.

It may go easily without saying that the remainder of
the night is somewhat blurred and indistinct. I wake
in a spartan little box-room on a Futon with Karen,
who had, I dimly recall, attacked me with a most

unfeminine persistence until I submitted. Yes, that is the word.

I had sighed and told her, "I'm not easy, but perhaps I could be had."

And she had flashed her teeth ferally in the darkness and whispered, fiercely, "I'll be as gentle as a little bird." She lied.

Now she lies on top of the Futon, naked, wrapped up in a sheet, her aggressive homeliness fled. She looks more like an overgrown child, her face relaxed and her breathing deep and regular. She doesn't move when I slide away and leave.

Czepelewski's house seems to be an irregular assembly of weathered sections added on at different times, following the undulating lines of an anchored dune covered with a dense growth of Shore Pine, Coast Juniper, Blue Oak, Ilex Vomitoria and tangles of Coccoloba Uvifera. The inside seems to have no relation to the outside shape—what one can make out of it.

Presently I find the sea-light streaming in, and find Czepelewski lounging on an ocean-facing deck in a hammock, wearing white duck pants and a straw hat, sipping at an enormous iced drink of venomous green color. When I come out, he is aware of me, but gives no sign. On his chest is a tattoo, covering an area about two hands, of exquisite artistry—no long-wharf job—and as complicated as a Maori mask. It appears to be an owl, drawn not in the usual cartoon style of tattoos, but in an unidentifiable but unmistakably oriental manner. But in this owl there is nothing of the dreamy opiated east of mountains and waterfalls and falling leaves, but rather an emblem of the worst excesses of Bushido, combined with the unabashed devilworship of the remoter parts of Tibet. It spoke plainly of the unalloyed terror and silent lethality of these silent wardens of the night, and nothing at all of the cuddly-animal image which caricatured owls as furry old men who spouted platitudes, or figures on children's towels. It is so obvious I look away.

That's the correct response. Although nothing tangible happens, there is a sudden drop in tension, a sensation of having passed a test. A first step.

For a time, still remote, his thoughts somewhere far off, along the horizon line of blue-on-blue, Czepelewski says nothing; but eventually he ventures, "You've seen the satellite, of course."

"Yes. Many times. I got tired of looking."

"So has everyone else. A marvel, some said. Others called it a miracle. Still others spoke of benefits to mankind. Benefits! We used to call them 'Bennies' in the Army. And when they served cold chicken in box lunches, we called them 'Box-Bennies,' too. But for us nothing's changed. That's not the doorway to freedom, but the inner sanctum of what passes for the official religion." He stopped for a minute. "At any rate, no one sings about the experience."

I say, "We don't sing about it because we don't share it. You have to communicate . . . that means shared experiences we can code down and remind them of."

"So it stays the same: Love and betrayal, the leaders are assholes, the thrill of the rush, good times of singing and dancing."

I say, "Did you ever write about it?" I understand why Kim reacted to him as she did; he talks like her—bizarre, flickering images, one after another, barely controlled. Nevertheless I understand his meaning perfectly. I share it. I just don't feel so strongly about it.

He says, "Sometimes. One about Mars, when they found out it was a rocky little desert, thin air and cold, nothing for us. What they did was praiseworthy, never take it away, but still our dreams were important. We would find the Mars we'd dreamed somewhere. Another about how they'd never send a cigarette poet up to gasp and marvel and *tell us what it's really like.* So."

"They land on the moon, but they don't sing blues to it."

"Exactly. But no one stands still, remains the same, and so we leftovers went on new paths, or do you follow that?"

"We took what was left. Used it our way."

"Yes. But the music you use is a frozen medium, invented fifty years ago. Frozen. But even with that, so far it's outlasted every other form, spread all over the world. But inside, there are no limits. What would you give to learn?"

"I won't give you my bass: it's an O'Hagen Shark with a two-octave fretless neck, damn near one of a kind. And I won't give you Kim because she's not mine to give."

He makes a subvocal bass grumbling deep in his throat, something between a growl and a chuckle. And says, "The best things come only once. Only once. Tonight, after you finish at the Mingo. On the beach, up toward Torre Quemado. Come and see. Perceive.''

"Why me?"

"You must learn that."

"What about Penderecky? Deligny? Tololo? Yiva Dandim?''

He shrugs. "They already know what is in them, the open spaces, the way to the secret journey."

"All right. Alone?"

"Bring whomever you will." At the end, he seems vastly indifferent. And whatever he has in mind, it isn't a casual pickup, nor a rendezvous. I look away, down the surf-line of the fading afternoon, and consider, trying to decipher Czepelewski's crypticisms . . . When I look back, he's gone. He hadn't made a sound or any motion I had noticed.

It turned out that Tololo had vanished as well, sailing off into the burnished afternoon in a sand-skimmer, a sort of catamaran with wheels. Karen, the all-purpose housekeeper, fixes a simple supper for us, while we all sit in corners or wander around dazed, like survivors. Kim reads from one of Czepelewski's books with an owlish concentration, which would be comical if she weren't so serious.

At dusk, when the light has fallen, Karen goes out to the garage and starts up the "Furry," and drives us all back to Pack's Landing, on the beach, of course, but this time at a more sedate pace. Now we can make out some of the passing scenes as we glide by, engines muffled and silent as a submarine on the hunt. Here, more of the beach houses are elegant, inhabited by languid, graceful pleasure-seekers now beginning their evening rites: some sip at drinks in tall glasses, while others fly kites of odd and variable shape in the evening breezes, darting and gliding in the violet upper airs. Others stand out on platforms and gesture at the sky, full of the panoply of old rose, gold, violet colors painted on the cirrus, pointing out particularly artful combinations of color and form. The men wear striped caftans with hoods, creatures of mystery, while the women wear voluminous flowing robes, which, rippling in the stirring of the air, suggest shape and form within, now revealed, now invisible, the artifact of the shadow of a shadow.

The elegant cottages, however, grow fewer, and finally end altogether, and large vacant tracts appear, and then, more houses, these older and plainer, lacking fancy name-boards or redwood stairs down to the surf. The outskirts of Pack's Landing.

Karen lets us off, subdued and silent, at the pier. When I go around to the front to thank her, I find her sitting in the tiny control cab, looking like some variation of a fighter pilot in a war that never was. Instruments, harnesses, coveralls, goggles. Aside from the night vision they gave her, what else did she see? She leers and flashes her feral smile, full of teeth, and growls, "Want some more?" When I hesitantly nod, she leans back, laughing, and turns the Furry around, to head off back down the beach, working the engine up through the gears, fading into the murk and vanishing. There were no running lights, and the machine makes no noise, leaving. It is eerie to see such a large machine move so silently.

The night's show goes poorly, slack, as if something had unraveled, somewhere out of sight. We act like a girl whose panty elastic has just snapped. Of course the audience senses it; they are telepaths in that and always have been. They aren't rude—just unfocused. Small conversations coalesce and dissipate, roiling along the edge of the dance floor like summer clouds. In desperation we call for requests, which serve for a time to head things off, but it is difficult struggling through unrehearsed by-guess-and-by-God arrangements.

After a time, we recover somewhat, and return to our own material. Kim takes the vocal on an old blues number we have, but rarely do, called, "My Man is Plannin' Evil."

"My man is plannin' evil—
You'd be evil, too.
I said my man is studyin' evil—
You'd be evil, too.
Since he turned against me
I don't know what I'm gonna do."

Suzanne does "Down in Mexico," and I do "Smoky Joe's Cafe," and we follow those with "Poke Salad Annie" and "Ain't no Call For Good Old Boys." But however much we think of recovery, we know it's just escape, and we close the set out with "Sweetest Apple on the Tree."

*   *   *

Outside, in the soft sand behind Lillie Mae's, we find
the soft, smudged prints of enormous balloon tires,
and a lingering faint scent of kerosene fumes. But
nothing else, and we do not comment on this. We all
go to our places in the house and crawl into empty
beds, alone and in silence.

But after a time, when the house has become
completely quiet, I get up and cross the dark, broken
by patches of light from the streetlamps, and slip out,
like a ghost, sure no one sees me. At the foot of the
stairs, though, there waits a figure in the shadows,
the dark fluff of her hair, the slender body clothed in
a flowing djellaba. Kim. This time, like conspirators,
we do not speak, but she holds out her hand, and I
take it. It is cool and dry. Silently, we cross the road
in the empty night to the beach, the surf sound
growing as we approach it. We turn left, toward
Torre Quemado, moving together as if we were one;
perhaps for a fleeting moment, we are. We glance at
each other from time to time: we are both guilty and
innocent.

Beyond Pack's Landing, after a while the houses
thin out, and there are some tidal marshes and inlets
before Torre Quemado proper. The tide is out, and
we walk through the warm water. Far ahead, we can
make out the lights of Cayo Ameca, more piers,
amusement parks, bars and clubs. But here it is
empty and dark, shifting land no one claims save the
beach-crabs. And just past the inlets, we stop, as if
obeying the same impulse and turn to each other, and
Kim undoes the single fastening and lets the cloth
unwrap and slip to her feet, stepping out of it, pale

lean body. I also, and like sleepwalkers we lie down together on the clothes and take each other fiercely, without apologies, without words, reaching just once more for the sweetness at the end of the rainbow, the ultimate erotic essense of which the body is only a mask, something beyond mere flesh, and once, for the asking, it's there, so easily and it doesn't end: we stop it.

And then? And then? We put our clothes back on, and resume walking toward whatever awaits us, up toward Torre Quemado.

Earlier, there had been some low-moving clouds, puffy and indistinct, scudding inland; now across the unseen sound, over the mainland, horizon lightning flickers and stabs silently, and occasionally the creamy domes of lightning-illuminated thunderstorms stand upright in frozen stroboscopic postures. Over us, the stars are out. Still sharing, we look up, into the depth of the night sky, and all of it is there, all the worlds and places and strange cities we'll never see, never know. There are no moving lights and shapes in that sky. The Satellite is elsewhere tonight. Up ahead a little, silhouetted against the weak ground glow from the beach towns, lies the jagged, harsh shape, low and rakish, like a pirate galley. Czepelewski's crane, with its canopy gone, the support poles and guys removed. Only the protruding control cab, out in front of the wheels, and the deck. It does not look quaint or arty or eccentric at all, but menacing and dangerous. There are no lights or movement.

Czepelewski waits for us on the beach. He begins,

ignoring the fact that there are two of us. "The way of the honor is one of will, choice and splendor; not survival or victory at any price, but above all, honor. Technology magnifies man, makes the road of accomplishment—admittedly difficult—easy, open to anyone, even totally dishonorable creatures. Did not the Shoguns of Japan know this, when they forbade firearms, and their samurai agreed? Technology magnifies, liberates, but without the discipline, what emerges? Men who are individually diminished. And so now is the age of wonders for the few, but they are diminished men and women, not heroes, but the slugs and the bugs." He glances up, theatrically. "Those creatures up there, spending years on the eye—are they men and women of honor, or are they children of the worm? We dreamed space as the last adventure and the greatest, a hundred years of song and story, but all fiction. The people up there are not the dreamers or the adventurers, but something else entirely. Perhaps the first; but less and less with each new generation. These now are professional poohs, a groomed elite, every wrinkle ironed and smoothed, totally trustworthy."

Kim says softly, "As powerless as us; they trust them because they have sold everything to them. They ignore us because we are powerless to interfere with or alter their schemes."

I say, "This is a phase, a part of it. The ships are, in actual fact, primitive compared to what they might be, and the knowledge involved questionable, hedged in a net of a thousand priorities. We speak too soon. What you're talking about is more revolutionary and more . . . mysterious, than anything ever attempted before. I'm dissatisfied, too, but I also understand that. . . ."

He makes a short, chopping gesture, and stops me. "No. It's not just another movement outwards. The difference is the reliance, or more properly, the addiction we have developed, for technology instead of our own resources. The more you rely on it the more you need. There's been a wrong turning."

"What can you do?"

"Not build gimcrack contraptions and pursue crackpot inventors! No! We go back farther than that, a lot farther." I can feel his intense persona focusing on me, not entirely sane as we might define sanity.

I say, "You'd wind up with people hopelessly out of touch with the world as it is. So self-directed they might be seen as—well, insane, and pushed even farther away."

He doesn't react with anger, but proceeds calmly, "Every person is an expression of the public and the private, but where sanity is discussed, we speak of a private internal reality we only assume we know. What we call insanity is nothing more than a set of internal references we neither perceive nor agree with. Only that. Examined dispassionately, the core ideas of the insane are no more ludicrous than the central dogmas of the sane. Some of them may be right, and us wrong . . . full of worth beyond any conception we might have . . ."

I interrupt, "And some of them are hopeless basket cases, too. They no longer function as independent members, but have to be cared for, their lives regulated."

"What are those lives on the Eye, but totally regulated, Cared for? Wards of the state, with a destruct button at every controller's desktop!"

Trapped. I say nothing.

He says, "We choose the safe way always. But only in risk does the glory lie. They have filled Earth with braying bureaucrats and space with mindless technicians, and the common man exercises his feeble remaining mind contriving ways to obstruct the flow for a moment so someone will notice him."

For a moment, my thoughts had synched up with his, and I could follow his current with my own memories, of thousands of ciphers, swallowed beyond recall, reduced to making pains-of-the-ass of themselves so that they might become visible, noticed, worth something. For a second. And granted the truth of it, to what end did Czepelewski aim? Music was close enough to chaos for me, and I feared and respected its powers. Czepelewski was toying with chimeras all history had devoted itself to eradicating from the collective consciousness. Then to face unknowns like that, you would indeed have to become . . . what? A warrior of sorts. Yes. That, first.

As if divining, partially, what was passing in my mind, he says, "I want no disciples, no followers. I offer this to those who may find use of it. I give it away. Now." He steps back, as if clearing a space between himself and us, raises his arm, which is covered by what seems to be a heavy welder's glove, and out of the night, silently, with no warning, a shape unfolds out of the darkness and settles on his gloved hand, closing its enormous wingspan. Kim grasps my hand convulsively, and her hand is clammy and cold. And I feel a sharp rush of an irrational fear I could only recall from farthest childhood, when I couldn't pass in front of a darkened garage without steeling myself against the consuming fear that something unspeakable was hiding there in the darkness. My tongue freezes in the roof of my mouth.

In the night light, at first it is impossible to discern any recognizable shape, and I am ready to believe in demons, familiars and other night-frits, but slowly, slowly, the thing takes on shape and outline, line and substance, emerging form: it is an Owl. But not of any species I know. This one seems as large, maybe larger, than an Eagle. Its talons are bare. Czepelewski offers it something, a little tidbit, with his free hand, which it takes and swallows complacently. He makes small chuckling, clicking noises to it, and it answers, muttering softly resonantly. I ask, "What have you been doing?"

"Selecting, enhancing, emphasizing. And from this and others we learn, one at a time. Learning to hunt the night. The day has become filled with dinosaurs. We made a daylight of technology, but we never escaped the dark nights. And those daysiders— they do nothing for *that*. They take your allegiance, but when you call on them, they answer, 'It's your personal problem!' So I have become an owler, and now I learn."

For an instant I see in my mind's eye a sorcerer, a magus, accompanied by the ever-present familiar; but that was something out of the far past, perhaps a past that exists only in fiction, in our imaginations. And yet, here, now: certainly nihilism, anarchy, and owls, from whom Czepelewski purchased the secrets of the night and with his poet's alchemy turned them into awful truths.

He continues, "Superb eyesight, coupled with an aural rangefinder; soundless wings, designed by relentless evolution for maximum lift, and muffled to make passage silent. Talons to catch, beak to kill quickly, and a powerful digestive system to make quick work of it. And at night, when the rest stumble and sniff along. Think of it! The lovely forms of the deer were shaped by the teeth of wolves. And what unknown forms do the owls sculpt?"

Kim hiccoughs and blurts out, "Paranoids!"

I say, "You have others, not just this one."

"I have others. The stock for this type, others as well, for more specialized purposes. But their purpose is to teach, as I adapt them to fill in the corners we have left. The light is for the heroes, and when they left, the real light went with them. We are now creatures of the darkness and the shadows, whether we know it or not. There were creatures in that darkness when we left it, and we have forgotten them, but now we rediscover the real perils."

I say, "It's a way, I can see that much of it. But it's a long way back, that darkness-before. We have forgotten much."

"I didn't make the dark. I didn't help them forget, either. Of such uses is a poet fitted in this day."

I say, "I too wince at the praised failures who

daily sell us all out for nothing more than their retirement plans—the lifers.''

He says, "I couldn't have said it better. So why waste time making music about the problem? You know it. That's just a buyoff from them, a little escape, lets them have room to fall back into it again. No—they're just prey.''

I say, "A lot of good and beautiful will go away.''

"Survivors have their unattractive aspects. But one can learn to appreciate functionalism.''

"Karen.''

"An excellent student. She will surpass me.''

I remember the enormous eyes, the wide, tooth-bared mouth, the power she held me in. And against that I contrast Kim's soft flowerpetal mouth, the gullwing curve of her eyebrows, the catch deep in her throat, the look of mingled submission, fear, and also triumph and desire in her eyes. The light in her eyes, coming and going lazily. Yes, and yes, also I would like to make their eyes water, too, but there was something more than sorcerous and repellent about what Czepelewski offered. The image returned of the warlock and his familiar, to whom he was ultimately in bondage. Czepelewski didn't own the owls he loved: they owned him.

"No.''

"Just like that,'' he scoffs.

He steps back, raises his arm slightly, and the owl spreads its enormous wings and takes to the air, silently, with hardly more than a puff of air to mark its going. Czepelewski says, "Currents of air, spiral whorls left in passing, that's all we ever know of each other, as close as we get.''

I touch Kim's hand and squeeze it, and she squeezes back. Not so—we had touched, more than currents and whorls—or if they were, they had stirred us mightily. I say, "It's not final. Just choice before I'm ready for such choices.''

But he is turning already back to the dune where Karen waits in his strange pirate ship, on the wheels and underframe of a mobile crane. He says, over his shoulder, "Of course not. Nothing's final—or everything is. And the only choices that matter are the very ones we never prepared for, never imagined. You only know what you miss when it's too late to catch up to it. But there's time, and so consider.''

I turn to Kim. "Come on. I'm tired, now.''

For a moment she stands, following him with her eyes as he trudges up the long sandy path back to the crane, and then she turns and comes with me. For a long time we don't look back, rather like Lot and wife leaving Sodom, but eventually we both look back. There is nothing there. We walk back to Pack's Landing holding hands, and when we reach the beach house, we lie down together, sleeping on our sides, facing each other, entwining our right arms with our woven fingers pressed to each other's mouth.

Awake; brazen, glassy afternoon, nobody in the house but me. I shower, rummage for something to eat, and then walk out into the shimmering peach light to have a look at Pack's Landing. The amusement park is lifeless, save for a scattering of urchins, tanned

uniform brown, and except for the water-slide, which
is filled with curious couples—beautiful, heartbreak-
ing young girls accompanied by hulking louts and
oafs, who seem much too old for the girls, glowering
cretins with premature potbellies fuelled by endless
beers which they swill evilly from sweating cans; the
Zoo Baba looks like an abandoned warehouse. Lillie
Mae's stands empty, a hulk, a husk, a loudspeaker
hanging on one rusty nail braying out moldy-oldies to
the empty street, cracked and bubbling in the heat,
There is clearly nothing happening in Pack's Landing,
never had, never could be. For a moment, like vertigo,
I lose what little nerve I have, the only thing that can
motivate you to walk out in awful places and face
awfuller crowds, night after night. *Why had we come
here?* We could have taken second billing and opened
for Cloven Hoof down in Coquina Pass.

Dusk, and then twilight: no breeze, and the sullen
heat remains. The light in the sky slowly evolves
from peach through blown rose into oily film. The
surf is lifeless and silent. I wait on the porch for the
others, watching the beach strip slowly come back to
life as the night people begin to emerge, first as
scattered singles, then couples, and small groups begin to form in the simmering chemistry of the endless
search for fulfilled desire, hunting for a thrill as they
once hunted for food in the vanished years of long
ago. The cunning gonads.

There's a haze in the air, and the stars don't come
out. Far off in the west there is something shining,
moving slowly and deliberately, planes and patches

of reflected sunlight. E-one. *There* they are going through their routines, chatting on the radio with their controllers, running checklists, reading instruments, perhaps even gazing at the stars they can see even in daylight. Most times we can't see them well at night.

Presently I recognize Pablo's rolling, easy amble as he strolls in from somewhere down the beach; musing, lost in reverie. Even from here I pick out the droopy, Mexican-bandit mustache he wears with fine indifference. He looks up, expecting me to be there, looks off again, crossing the street. I know: I'm not real—only women and music.

As Pablo joins me on the porch, Suzanne turns into the yard from around the corner of Lillie Mae's, dressed in her favorite summer things, a white tube top and a loose, gauzy skirt which for an instant the streetlights from the beach road shine through from behind. She climbs the stairs, wooden clogs bumping on the wooden treads.

Pablo says, into the stifling night, "I thought your Momma taught you you'd never sneak in wearing those clogs."

"Most of the time, you guys wouldn't notice anyway. And if I was sneaking, I'd come barefooted and you'd never hear a thing." Suzanne stands behind me and I can breathe her scent of sun and skin and suntan oil, and the dry cotton of her skirt. Beautiful, and not for us. She steps out of her clogs and slips inside the house brushing her hand across my shoulders as she goes; nothing special. Just contact.

Last, as always, Rommy comes trudging up the

driveway, carrying a surf-fishing pole, smelling of
fish and salt water and the fine, pungent onion odor
of sweat. We ask, lamely, "Catch anything?"

"Nah!", he calls up disgustedly from the drive.
"Threw all of them back." He comes up on the
porch. "Saw something odd a while back, though."

"What's that?"

"Saw Czepelewski's party wagon, but all stripped.
It was here. I was over across the street, wuffin'
down a tube-steak. Turned in, stayed a while, and
then left. The sun was wrong on the windows, and I
couldn't see who was in it. It wasn't his gun-bearer
come cattin' for you, was it—that overalls-girl?"

"Not me! I had a rough night and slept it off all
day."

"Where's Kim?"

"I don't know. When I woke up, the house was
empty." It was then that I remembered to worry.
Only then. We would be on in an hour or so at Lillie
Mae's, and nobody knew where Kim was. "I thought
she might have wandered off with one of you."

Rom scratches his beard, and muses aloud, "Wandered off, so much I can believe. One of us? Not
Pablo. He's got a main squeeze stashed down the
beach. He left right after I did, early; can you stand
it? And you know Suze . . . she wouldn't go to a
dog-fight with Kim offstage." He stopped, as if the
same thing occurred to him as to me. "Are we on the
verge of having a problem?"

"Maybe." Kim had more than once been irresponsi-
ble and was prone to wander off, and had done so
often, immersed in some subterranean private fantasy.

We all kept an eye on her, because if Suzanne finished and polished the music, and made us rehearse, then it had always been Kim who had been our window into chaos. As André Gide said—"Reason writes what madness prompts." I say, "No point in going off half-cocked and bass-ackerds: she could be anywhere."

Rom nods, barely moving. "Yeh. Well, maybe she'll remember what time it is. Opening time is the only time you ever have to worry about."

But opening hour comes and goes and there is no sign of Kim. Rommy ambles down to Lillie Mae's to stall off the man for a while, but even with that, there's no avoiding it. The contract says a quintet, with all members functional.

Midnight comes. At Lillie Mae's, they are sympathetic, even buying us a round of drinks, but in the end they pay us off and throw us out. Twenty-four hours to clear the house. They had already replaced us with a "new-wave" band from the Zoo Baba, across the street, who call themselves Samurai Chiropractor. Their show is called, "A Night of Bushido." Even when we go back to the house we can hear the din. It is appalling. They only know one time signature, 4/4, and two keys, C and F. We can't make out the lyrics, thank God.

Rommy settles ponderously into a deck chair and props his feet up on the rail, holding a beer long since gone stale. He says, "For a moment, I had hopes we had educated those people to 9/8 time." It's a lame remark and we let it lie and die of its own accord. Suzanne goes in the house and goes to bed, and Pablo sidles off, sheepishly, obviously going looking for his squeeze.

After a long time, I say, "I know where she went."

Rom: "Will you go after her?"

"Yes. But I have no way, now. They won't come after me . . ."

"There's always a way. May take some time."

"You're not going."

"Somebody has to make arrangements."

"You're a mother hen, you know?"

"Yeh. But this is something only you can do. Forget Twilight's Last Gleaming, man. Just get her back."

"Sure." I get up and start down the stairs. "Take care of my bass, will you?"

Rom nods. "The old locker at Emerald Music, up in Cayo Ameca. The same old combination."

I start walking. It's a long way to Cochicabamba, and I've got plenty of time to sort things out. What I should say, and what I shouldn't; and how in the dawn of the age of space there's no handy pushbutton way to get a girl back save by the ancient and honorable way of walking in the night. The real problems they haven't even begun to sort out, much less solve, and the stuff they have done isn't much more than a set of high-grade toys. But that's Czepelewski's line, and I'm agreeing with the evil sorcerer even as I go charging off to leap into his castle and save the maiden. Only Kim is no maiden, and Czepelewski's no sorcerer: I don't believe in sorcerers. Simple. But it helps to imagine him that way. However it's a lot farther walking than it had been, riding. The houses draw back from the water on my right, and the tide falls away on my left, and Cochicabamba seems to get no nearer. And in fact, it doesn't seem to look any different than the rest of the beach. But the shore dunes are getting higher, more of the vegetation on them, and they seem to roll and pitch more. A-frames, geodesic domes, glass houses. I wonder, *Suppose I can't find it?* and Then, *Suppose it isn't there anymore?*

I stop to try to make out the outlines of the erratic structure I'm looking for, or the wind-chime pylon, and I sense motion, gone before I can properly locate it. I have a sudden prickly sense of intense attention, and look around, down along the ground, and behind me sits quietly Czepelewski's remodeled crane, slowly inching forward, absolutely silent.

I stop and wait for it, and presently it glides slowly to a stop beside me. Even next to it, I can hardly hear the engine—a distant burry mumbling, somewhere else. The door lock releases and the window slides down. Soundlessly, except the click of the door. Karen. With her mixed-vision driving goggles on. She does not look quite at me, but I understand that she sees me. "Get in. You passed it twenty minutes ago."

"How do you know that's where I'm going?"

"What the hell else would you be doing walking to Cochicabamba? I've had you in sight for three hours, and damn tiring it's been, too."

I get in. "If you knew, and were there, why not just give me a ride?"

"That's not the way. You have to make your own steps. Now you've made enough. We don't play with people."

She swings the machine around, easily, still silently, and for a short time we roll along the beach, and then turns in, onto a track into the dunes that looks like no more than a path. The crane wallows a little and plows easily through the soft, dry sand. Karen says, as if talking to herself, into the close air of the cab, "She's here, of course, we're not holding her. She'll see you—might even still want you. Those things don't change, just the ways they can manifest themselves. The way things were, you never had a chance. You were in the wrong world in your heads."

That's all she says. The machine glides under a dense canopy of Live Oaks, pressed and stretched into fantastic shapes by the sea winds, and lent horrific illumination by the lights of the machine. Under a wooden catwalk, and into a cavernous overhanging shed. Karen carefully shuts the machine down, and closes the door behind us.

She gets out and motions me to follow. Still wearing those shapeless coveralls, barefooted, walking silently, with a dancelike gliding motion I hadn't noticed before. There is a spiral staircase, white stucco, going up and up, a long way before there are any landings, lit by small footlights. The few that are there she ignores and continues all the way to the top, where the spiral opens out into a spacious cupola, open to the air and the winds, screened off from

below by a dense jungle of live oaks and beach
junipers. There is an overcast daylight, deep blue
yet, and the ocean is glassy and greenish. And Kim
is there, sitting with her legs stretched out on one of
the benches that follow the curve of the rail, now
looking out over the sea. Overalls satisfies herself
that everything is arranged as it's supposed to be, and
then fades back down the spiral.

Kim is wearing a faded sweatshirt and a loose pair
of pants, and when she turns from the ocean and to
me her face is full of an expression I'd only seen in
glimpses before. I say, "I was worried about you."

"And so now you are here. I'm fine—not to worry.
Both of us are here."

"I suppose there's no need to ask you to come
back."

"You could ask, but I won't come; but there's no
malice in it, nothing bad. It just had to be this way: I
saw and I knew. There was no point in making a
scene. Here, sit with me." She extends her hand,
delicate and pale, bordered by those close-chewed
fingernails I know so well. And her face; there's no
anger in it, not even determination, but a tremendous
tenderness. I sit, and she takes my hand, shyly, like a
child.

I say, "I think I understand you now less than I
ever did."

"It's hard to say it rightly, you know; everything
real is hard to put into words, and the stuff that goes
into them easily isn't worth fooling around with.
Sometimes you have to give up and feel around the
edges, like with music. But in the end that too is just

another way of avoiding things, the way we all did it. The world isn't right, but we were escaping instead of changing. You see? The sensitives see it first, and they run from it."

I say, "I remember. We went over this one night long ago with a pillow between us. We can't change it. It's built so outsiders can't get in unless they become insiders. You get railroaded into the proper categories long before you are even aware you could have a choice in such things."

"And so all we have left is to sing about it. And all those people who listen to us, dance before us— what do they do? Tonight they grope, clasp each other, dance and sing, and tomorrow they walk right back to Pharoah, building pyramids to dead kings. I know it, you knew it. I was drowning in it."

"So what more can you do from here?"

"Collect, instead of scattering. Unravel, instead of buying it off with an anodyne. Build, work. Pick locks and pull down walls. We never see what's around us except through an interior landscape we never question; we're going to teach people how to ask the right questions. That's why this is worth doing: we don't know what the answers will be, so the questions stop being rhetorical posturings, and we can't fail because we anticipate nothing."

"You're talking about . . . a lot of time. You and I will never see the answers."

"That's the problem that always held us back, when anyone tried this before. We wanted results for us, now. But truth is that in all things we who make a thing cannot possess it. Faith and belief, will and idea. Slow and right at first, only at the end does everything come together right. Love is that way." She hasn't so much changed, as taken a part of herself that only slipped out in flashes before, and given it freedom. What she is saying doesn't lack for radicality, but it's totally her own, and there's no trace of Czepelewski in it.

She goes on, "And so people come here to escape for a while, leave their grinds inland; here they live differently. They swim, sail, fish, dress provocatively, dance, enjoy, endure the changing ocean and the sand and the sulfurous water. But the real truth is that these lives here are the reality, and it's their grind routines that are unreal! What little reality we have is here, and from here we are going to put it back into the collective mind, root it in reality. Only then can the real adventurers make space their own. What's there now are only fragments of an evil dream."

"If I grant that you can change it, maybe by then they won't want to."

She shakes her head, moving the soft exploded curls. "No. Life always moves uphill into more difficult environments, upstream."

"This doesn't sound like you so much, but it isn't him, either."

She presses my hand. "That's a me I'm just learning to let speak. A me you don't know so well. You could get to know her too." She stops a moment, and then adds, "And so this is more demanding. But you could. I know the things you think, however well you hide them."

"That's true, but I don't know if I can share you."

She leans to me and brushes my face with hers, lightly. "That's the worst mistake any of us ever made. We will all share each other, eventually. You don't stop loving someone when you come to love others. That's the way we really are. It was added-on that you have to reject."

I know that what she's saying is true, in that hallucinating way she has. I say, "But I don't know if I can endure it."

"To learn is pain, sometimes, and other times you just catch on, instantly, and then spend the rest of your life trying to string it out in a line so it makes sense. It's like I told you: this unreality problem goes back a long, long way. It's all in his notebooks, along with the terrible cynicism he puts on in public. The mistake occurred in classical Greece, in a very specific year, in a specific number of people whose names are all known. One tiny turn, right there—but it changed, then and there. Like fire, they brought a dangerous gift. What they did was already out of control by the time of Jesus. He saw it with the wisdom of the old world they had destroyed, and gave the remedy—"love each other"—only that. But it was too late *then*. All things have their cure. We just had to wait until now."

"I don't believe you've become a cellar-christian."

"No. The people who followed him were all wholly of the new order. It's now that it's running out of steam. Don't you understand that the real truths liberate us, not bind us? But those Greeks who changed it—they didn't know what they were doing. We do. And in time we'll undo what they did and set it right.

This isn't politics and it isn't religion. Politicians: afterwards, we'll keep a few, the way they keep rare animals in preserves.''

I say, ''And we'll have shamans, and witch doctors, and sorcerers like Czepelewski.''

''It's not Science we're fighting, but the idea that Science isn't an art.''

Once again she had slipped ahead of me and waited for me to come to her. ''What about Twilight's Last Gleaming? Suzanne, Pablo, Rom?''

''They'll find someone else. In their world, everyone's replaceable. If everything else fails, they'll sing someone else's music.''

''How the hell did he pick you?''

Now she lowers her head, curiously submissive, for the first time hiding her chocolate eyes. She answers softly, almost inaudibly, ''It wasn't me he chose. It was you. I saw that, that he'd never reach you. This was my idea, not his. I came, to bring you.''

It hits me like a fist, a flash of lightning. Now I see all of it, what I had been refusing to see all along. She looks back up at me directly, into my eyes and beyond, and says, still in that hushed voice, husky with unshed tears, ''I gave you to Karen, not the other way around.''

I let that sit for a long time. ''And what do we do while we're waiting for the Revolution?''

''That's where the rest come in: Penderecky, Deligny, Tololo, Dandim. Jobs, income, survival. And time to live, too. We'll give up a lot of the old and a lot of what we thought we wanted, but I don't

have to be crazy anymore, spaced, freaked. I'm going
to learn to harness it.''

"What do I learn?"

"How to release what's in you that you don't
know—or fear."

I nod, slowly, something slowly coming into view.
"When I have been able to really get into the music,
I mean, let it control me, I feel as if there was
another me there—a better one, I might add; not the
same old usual one I see in the mirror."

She says, "That's the secret: the one you fear to
let out is the one others see, value. Love. And that
one's got something to say. That's what he wants.
That we stop living in the mirror."

"It's a lot to accept at one bite."

She knows that's what I'd say. I can see her follow
me perfectly, by little inclinations of the head, eye
motions. She answers, "Go back down the beach
and get your Bass. You don't have to give up anything.
What you can do . . . what we can do." I squeeze
her cool hands and bend over to brush her eyelids in
a light kiss that is all affection.

"Don't worry. I'll be back."

I feel my way down the spiral into the cool creo-
sote dimness and damp of the garage, where Czepelewski's absurd machine looms like some prehistoric
monster, which it is. Lurking in its cave. But I lean
on it, image or no, for it is also just a machine, now
inactive, the magic gone out of it, the life in
suspension. And I find the door to the outside, where
the cool blue early morning overcast has brightened
up to rose-gray, and where in the tangles of scrub

oak and oleander the insects are starting to chatter and drone.

Palmyra Sound, Coquina Pass, Turquoise Island Beach and all its string of indistinguishable beach towns: Pack's Landing, Tusuque, Trocadera, Cayo Ameca, Cochicabamba, Rivadavía, Flor de Luna, Cerro Gordo, Arrirang, Torre Quemado, Mutiny Point, Cabo de Las Perdidas. The future is here, but the beach goes on forever, the names changing but not the realities underlying the names.

Afterword: I met the idea underlying this tale first in 1962 in Eugene, Oregon. I am much indebted to Larry Setnosky, who suggested it, and also to the works of Robert Pirsig, which helped focus it better.

LEANNE

As most working writers have learned by bitter experience, stories which come complete are rare; they come in pieces and have to be laboriously stitched together in most cases. Therefore, if by chance one should catch one of these infrequent visitors, one should take it as it is, and worry afterwards how exactly to categorize it. Curiously, although this story "came complete as is," I cannot remember exactly when it occurred to me; it might have been sometime during the summer of '82 but, equally probable, it might also have fallen out of space a lot further back, and lain quietly about, waiting to be used. I believe that one has to use material like this, or lose the ability to hear it at all.

For J. Gentry.

Morgan closed the door to his apartment and locked it. Before closing the inside-only deadbolt, he called out, to find out if Tierney was home. There was no answer. He left the door as it was, so the boy could get back in when he came home.

As if Tierney's absence reminded him, Morgan reflected on his son. He knew that all his efforts to date had proven useless. Was it Tierney's fault, or flaws, or those of the world they lived in? You couldn't answer such questions. What you could do was point out what had to be done, like it or not. But there, too, how far could you go? You could explain, verify, demonstrate alternatives, explain consequences. But in the end you could not live one second of another's life for him, even your own son's.

It was not simple; Tierney was neither stupid, obstinate, nor lacking in ability. Quite the contrary. As a fact, Morgan thought highly of his son, and valued him above all the other accomplishments and events of his life. It was a problem that seemed to have no solution; indeed, it caused Morgan to question the things he tried to persuade Tierney to do, or become. Perhaps Morgan was wrong. And so perhaps Tierney was right.

The boy was something of a dreamer. But it went deeper than that. Deep down, where everyone knows the truth, he *knew* he was wrong, and hence, Tierney right. There was no question about it. But what could one do? One inhabited a wrong world, and to survive in it, one had to partake of its wrongness. *Arrival of the fittest.* Thus you could scratch out a living. And you could be right, right indeed, and struggle uselessly, an insect caught in snares beyond its comprehension, or else swatted away as a nuisance, like the roaches in the bottom of the sink cabinet with whom Morgan shared a wary relationship.

And so, what about Tierney? Sensitive, gifted with insights Morgan couldn't remember having had, able to translate imagination into realities. But of course useless, useless. This was a world in which one survived solely upon one's willingness to do. Simple things, dirty things, obnoxious things. It was not a world which paid you for what you knew. Or could perceive.

Morgan hung his raincoat up and wandered into the kitchen, noting that the cooker was programmed and running. Tierney always did the little things effortlessly, claiming that he wanted to get them out of the way. And he thought it was good that the boy was out, learning, he hoped, how to tomcat around and steal a little joy. God knows, they wouldn't give you any.

He made a pot of tea, waited for the cooker to finish, and sat down to eat, letting the fatigue of the day sink in and come to rest. That was the way things were, too. You could run all day if you had to, and most had to, through one job in which they observed the letter of the wage laws and paid you the minimum, and through a second, equally righteous, by the end of which you had run up a long day indeed. And once you stopped running, then sleep claimed you. He glanced up at the flat kitchen light and nodded. Right. At least you didn't have to worry about insomnia. There could be something said for fatigue.

He finished and cleared the table. Portion meals,

nothing wasted, nothing to wash, all from the Bureau
of Nutriment. A line from an ancient song rattled
through his head:

> "TeeVee dinners by the pool;
>   Aren't you glad you finished school?"*

Morgan turned out the kitchen light and returned to
the living room, turning on the data terminal absentmindedly. When he had been growing up, they had
had newspapers, radio, TV. None of them had been
very good, but they were all so generalized that
something of the real stuff managed to slip through
once in a while. Now they had data terminals, now
there were two hundred channels, and they didn't call
it television anymore. All specialized subjects, twenty-
four hours a day, nonstop. Fifteen channels of sports,
ten of music, two soap operas, three weather channels.
Channels were also allocated to General Health, Sexual Adjustment, Current Economics, Military Actions and Civil Disorders, Disaster Command Post,
Crime and Punishment, Celebrity Doings, and Human Interest. *On top of it all*: the harder they spec-
tated the world, the more out of control and obnoxious
it became.

He held down the advance button and let it stop at
random. It stopped on Channel 129, Military Actions
and Civil Disorders, popularly called D & D. Now,
there was a good action channel: always something
going on in the world somewhere. Morgan settled

---

*Frank Zappa, *Brown Shoes Don't Make It*, Absolutely Free,
Third Story Music, 1969.

into his chair, waiting for the channel's self-promotional ad to finish.

This channel's central studio resembled a military command post, and all the announcers and staff were dressed in suitably denationalized camouflage fatigues. Cammos, they called them. A plain girl with steel-rim spectacles solemnly announced:

"The insurrection in Northern Nigeria continues at this hour, and for further progress reports we transfer you live by satellite to MAC/D's Local Command Post in Jos, Nigeria."

The scene flickered to a much plainer studio that had a temporary air to it, like some airlifted trailer. The announcer was a grim, expressionless man of no discernible race or age, accompanied by a black officer in a field uniform, who said nothing, but appeared to be watching a monitor off-camera intently. The announcer explained:

"The insurrection apparently began two weeks ago during a dispute over bus fares in the town of Fadan Karshe; shortly afterwards it was blown into a full-scale insurrection by local army defectors under Corporal Tsofo Bassa. This morning, events assumed a more serious cast when rebels moved out of their strongpoints in the Monguna Arna Hills and captured the junction of highways 86 and 104 west of Nimbia. The rebels are expected to move tomorrow northeast up highway 86 and attempt to block the railroad below Gawanuri. To date, the action has been

*contained by the local garrison from Panyam,
but reinforcements are reported moving up highway 108 from Langtang, as well as some light
armor from Lere. I have with me here a government spokesman, Major Nassarawa Mulfama,
who has more information to report.''*

The announcer turned to Major Mulfama, as the
scene faded into what appeared to be file footage of
the area. It was not the sort of Africa one might have
imagined from travelogues, but a hot, severe land of
yellowish hills broken up by house-sized boulders.
Where there was ground cover, it was dry and low
scrub. The sun blazed out of a sky of dusty pearl. To
one side ran a dried-up track that might be a muddy
runnel during the rainy season. An offscreen voice,
presumably Major Mulfama, cultured and careful, its
accent neutral, said,

*"This is typical terrain south of Jos. Al-
though it seems open, there is considerable cover
in those rocks for snipers. For the moment, we
intend to contain the rebels to this sector.
Hopefully, the reinforcements will be able to
move in, reopen the road, and begin dispersal
operations.''*

The terrain faded on the screen, first to a satellite
shot of the area, followed by a topographic map,
which faded into a computer presentation, indicating
as well the position of Kano, the nearest large city,
which was somewhat off to the northwest.

*   *   *

Morgan was yawning, but he was starting to get interested in the Tsofo Bassa Rebellion. That would be a good one—they would go on at length for at least half an hour, complete with interviews, action footage, and local color shots. Wars and rebellions always seemed to happen in the damnedest places, all of them with funny names. He wondered if the MAC/D people would act the same if Henry County, Virginia seceded from the Union. Probably would. It was all grist for their mill: only the backgrounds changed. In fact, he wouldn't have been at all surprised if some MAC/D people hadn't instigated the riot that had started it. But Morgan was not to complete that line of speculation, for the apartment door rattled, a key being inserted in the outside lock. Tierney.

Tierney was slighter of build than Morgan, even allowing for middle-age thickening and rounding; his face was more sharply defined, and in those things he shared his mother's genes. Her face; but an elusive part. Morgan could never be completely sure which part, because it shifted, according to the day. But Tierney never showed her shimmer of feral calculation. He looked at the world steadily, plainly.

Tierney said, "I'm surprised you're still up."

"I wouldn't have been for long. Besides, you're in early."

"Yeah. . . ." Tierney went into the kitchen, opening drawers, closing them, running water."

Morgan asked, "Did you turn up anything today?"

From the kitchen, Tierney answered, "Yes, and no."

"Want to tell me?"

"Not really."

Morgan knew his moods, and there was nothing to be gained in pushing him tonight. Whatever he had tried to do, it hadn't worked at night, either. Growing up was hard enough. He got up from the chair and said, "I'm off tomorrow. We can go do something."

Tierney stopped rummaging and looked out of the kitchen. "Did you really get both jobs off at the same time?"

"Yeah. Fluke of the skeds, but that's the way it fell." He didn't say any more. Let Tierney set it.

"What did you want to do?"

Morgan said, "Oh, nothing special. I didn't have anything in mind. You know you can't plan much, the way things are. You only know a day or so in advance—that way they keep you guessing. It's standard practice, so the executive trainees tell me."

"You mean the salesmen."

"Cold-calls and product knowledge and hard closers."

Tierney nodded at the cynicism, knowing it well by now, and said, "Wouldn't be a bad idea—just knock around a little. Maybe the zoo."

"Right. Now I'm going to bed. You going to stay up?"

"For a while. I'm working on something."

"Don't stay up too late."

"I won't."

*　　　*　　　*

The next morning Morgan came out into the living room and noticed, on Tierney's open work-desk, a simple object. It was a sculpted bust of a girl, in some pale, fine-grained wood. The bust wasn't yet finished; he could sense that. Tierney always finished his projects, whatever they were, with a sense of a hard line, a clear and crisp definition, and this one was still in the rough in some parts. But mysterious and compelling. The mouth was soft and indistinct, wide, easy to smile or to give sudden, impulsive wet kisses. The eyes were deepset, penetrating. Bold and gallant. Yes. Gallant. Morgan was sure that the bust had been done from life, but it was of no one he had ever seen or heard Tierney speak of. Maybe it was some girl he had seen passing on the Magel.

Later, riding downcity to the zoo on the same Magel, Morgan mentioned casually that he had seen the bust.

Tierney said, "Got the wood back when I had that temp roster job clearing some old shrubbery out. It's Ligustrum wood. Relative of the olive tree. Beautiful stuff, heavy and fine. No splitting. And getting rarer and rarer, in pieces big enough to work with."

"Who's the girl?"

"Oh, nobody; Lumen Parrie, girl at school."

He didn't volunteer anything else, and Morgan didn't ask.

Outside, it was winter, and the trees were bare. The sky was overcast, but there was no rain yet, although two of the three weather channels claimed there was supposed to be. It was damp, though, with a real bite

to the air. There weren't many people at the zoo, and
few of the animals were out. Except the polar bears.
Apparently they only felt at home when it was beastly
outside. Their enclosure was all rocks and water, and
they ambled around, in that aimlessly, potentially
violent way they had, looking for something to get
into, watching the people. They always watched the
people closely, as if they had been put there solely
for their entertainment. People were interesting; not
so much good as game maybe, but edible should they
happen to fall in the enclosure. Maybe some day . . .
They had plenty of time. Morgan mentioned this to
Tierney, guardedly, and Tierney laughed at the thought.

"Wouldn't that be something. Wouldn't surprise
me a bit."

"Ah, just a joke. Oldest one in the world, them
outside and us inside the zoo. They used to tell that
one all the time down by the Monkey house."

Tierney leaned on the rail over the Bear enclosure
and looked down at the three bears currently in sight.
After a long time, he said, "I did turn up something
yesterday."

Morgan sensed that it wasn't very good. "What
was it?"

"Cooker loader, third shift, down at General
Byproducts."

Morgan shook his head. "Jesus, a rendering plant.
You don't exactly look like you're filled with professional zeal."

Tierney said, "You ever been down there?"

"No. But I've heard plenty. It's a rendering plant—
animal carcasses, bad food, God only knows what

else they stuff in there. A fragrant pine forest it isn't."

"Smell is only the beginning. Everything's covered in grease, even the pavements. You have to walk just so or you fall in it. And the workers down there . . . You think they'd pay more, but they don't, and those people kind of shuffle around, like they've gotten used to it. They have a look in their eyes like they don't care anymore. Why wash it off, there'll just be more glop tomorrow."

Morgan shook his head. "You'd almost be better off in the Labor Pool."

"Yeah, but all these certificates I got from school, they don't seem to do any good. Those jobs are already filled, or else they tell me I'm overqualified. Whatever that means."

Morgan said, cynically, "It means no, only they don't have balls enough to tell you. No matter. Those kind of weasel people don't deserve good workers anyway."

"I just feel like I need to do something."

"Well, what you saw down there at the plant, I see every day, maybe not so drastic, but all the same. You just have it beaten out of you. The trouble is that it doesn't hurt much—just a little, every day, and some can take it and not change, but most do. People wind up looking like animals after a while, and at that the unpleasant ones. Saw a woman the other night on the way home who looked just like a hog, and she had a bad disposition, too. But look: granted all that, you still don't have to sign up for something that bad, do you?"

"I don't want it, but I feel like I should . . ."

"Forget it. Few people stick together anymore, so stay as long as you like and don't worry about it. You're not under real pressure yet. Let it come on its own time."

"That's okay, but even you said that a kid's got to get out on his own sooner or later."

"You're old enough to be told that parents say crap like that, thinking like they remember back when. That was a good idea once. Damn good idea. When I was coming along I couldn't wait to be off. Anything! But listen—it's not the same now. We've had all this change, but the world really hasn't gotten any better for the most of us, just regular people, raising kids and trying to get by. Oh, yeah—we got robots. They get the plum jobs, not the really shitty ones, which the people still do. And so today we've got all this stuff for entertainment like we didn't have then, but the hard line is that boredom doesn't have a bottom line, and it's just like poverty, throwing money at it doesn't cure it. And we've liberated ourselves from all that traditionalist bullshit, only now there isn't any slack at all, and all people say to each other is, 'like man, what's in it for me?' Everywhere. A lot of folks my age have kids still at home, plenty older than you."

"I read some of the stuff they used to think, and it's funny, in a way. They really thought it was almost within reach, and yet it's not turned out that way. We know. We talk about the good old days more than you do."

"Yeah, but you didn't know them. You had 'em

that way now, you'd do the same things we did. It all comes from not taking chances on the stuff we should, and reaching for what we can't handle. We get neither in the end." Morgan paused a minute. Then, "So you got a girl, you want a place to go, bring her in, just do it, don't worry about me. I'll give you room—you need it."

Tierney looked around sharply. "Assuming I could get one. But what about you?"

"Forget it. The ones I want, they don't want a two-job sugar daddy who rides the mag to work. I've learned to cope with it. It's always somebody handy, like close at the office, or some guy with a lot of flash. That's the way it's always been. The real thing is harder to find than a good job. And listen— everybody talks sex, but if everyone got all they claimed, we'd all walk around like a bunch of zombies. Believe that."

Tierney nodded, as if it was something he already suspected. Always somebody else! But after a time he said, "I have to tell you something."

"What?"

"You remember that dream I told you about?"

Morgan thought for a moment, and then said, "Something about a blonde girl in the woods. Yes, I remember."

"Nothing to it, except it wasn't in the woods, but in a kind of field, and she had a name: Leanne. But it wasn't the usual sort of dream you have, where everything is rubbery and changing. This was different. It ran just like real life. That's why I remembered it."

"I know those kind. Later, sometimes years later, you live through a small segment that you know you've been in before, word for word. Déjà vu. They have a name for it, but naming doesn't mean understanding. If you don't know it, you will find it out. And sometimes you have that kind of dream, the same kind, and nothing comes of it. You always lived in the city."

Tierney set his mouth a little harder. "If it was somebody I'd met, I'd know. I'd remember."

"Like I said, they don't know everything. They don't even know exactly what sleep is. Only that we need two different kinds of it—REM sleep, which is when we dream, and the other kind, when we don't. Maybe. Enjoy the good ones, forget the bad ones, it's just like real life."

"I had another one."

Morgan became more attentive, and less the gruff advisor. "Same girl?"

"Yeah, Leanne. Only this time we were older, not little kids anymore. Teenagers, sort of young. It was in the same kind of country as before. I remembered it. Near the same place. A lot of sky, grassy plains or prairies, and the land was broken up by a lot of small creeks and old canals. Old trees grew along the banks and hung over the water. People had houseboats on some of the wider ones. She came through the grass for me, that was the way it started, and it was like we remembered each other. We walked for a long time, just talking, and then we came to the houseboat, on a wide bywater along one of these canals, the old slow creeks. It was in summer, in the afternoon. We went swimming.''

Morgan asked, hating to intrude, ''How did you go swimming?''

''We took our clothes off. It seemed easy, natural. Nobody would mind. I knew this. We touched each other in the water, and then we climbed on the boat, and Leanne got us some towels to wrap up in, because it had gotten cooler. It does, there, in the evening. Uh, nobody was home but us, so after a while we. . . .''

Morgan said, ''It's only natural to have those kinds of dreams. Everybody does. Not to worry.''

Tierney shook his head. ''I know about *that*. This was different. It all happened in real time. No jumping around, no shifting. And in that kind of dream, you wake up. Afterwards, I didn't. And there were some things . . . I didn't know, that I knew were right afterwards. I couldn't have known them, except . . .''

Morgan looked at the bears. Overgrown dogs. He wondered if bears had dreams. Dogs did, because they ran and barked in their sleep, their barks coming muffled, like bubbles rising from under a log. Yes. He was sure bears dreamed. Of what? He said, ''Son, some of that knowledge is stored in instincts millions of years old; you don't have to learn it. It's already there. It's too important. The mind plays tricks and dresses it up for you.''

''No, this is real, somehow. I know it. It has the same ordinary feel as right here and now.''

''Okay. How did this one end, this time?''

"It was almost dark when we finished. We got dressed, and she said she had to go back this time, but that she would come back for me. As many times as it took. She repeated that. She told me that someday I could come to her, but not yet. Something—it was a word I don't know and can't remember—wasn't right yet."

"As many times as it took for what?"

"She didn't say, but there, then, I understood that she meant being there permanently."

Morgan chewed on his lip for a minute, and then asked, gently, "Do you want to go to counseling about this?"

"No. Do you think I ought to?"

"No, not really. You say it's the same world? You're sure?"

"It was the same world, the same place. I knew there was a city nearby. She was the same, but about five years older than the first dream I had, when we were just kids. No sex, then."

"Do you fear it? Her?"

"There's no fear there. I don't know how I know. I just know it. There's none in her."

Morgan knew that well enough. It was fear that made people act the way they did, stealing when they could have paradise just by asking the right way. Well, that opportunity had long since passed. He asked, "What does she call you?"

"My name. Tierney."

"Does she have a last name?"

"I have not heard one. I don't know."

"Where does she live?"

"In the city, mostly. I don't know how I know that. I just do."

"Does she come when you want her to come?"

"No. Only those two times. They don't happen because I want them to. They just happen, not tied to anything."

Morgan sighed, and looked back at the bears. He had expected something like this, sooner or later. But there was something about it that bothered him: Tierney believed it implicitly, and Morgan found himself half-believing it, too. It wasn't any sort of dreaming he'd ever heard of, but Tierney was convinced there was nothing to fear, and Morgan felt this, too, even at second hand.

The boy said, "Bats already, hah?"

"Doesn't sound like it to me. But I can't see any harm in it, yet, at any rate. Say, when you are *there*, do you remember *here*, or anything like that?"

"I remember here . . . and what I'm doing there, it's like I know it's something you'd want me to do."

"I'm trying to rationalize this from something of this world, but I'm damned if I can. But I still don't see any need to be afraid of it."

"Did you ever have dreams like that?"

"No, but I've had some strange enough, you can bet. Never mind. If you have any more of these, please tell me. Now—how about some real junk food! Down the road a bit there's a fine little stand, where you can get the worst hot dog in town. Tube steak would be good for you; one does not live by

Bureau of Nutriment Portion Control alone. Or something like that.''

Tierney, with Morgan's encouragement, did not take the position at General Byproducts. He signed up again for the labor pool temporary list, and went traveling around, doing all sorts of things. Sometimes he might be in when Morgan came home, other times, not. But after a time, Morgan noticed that Tierney didn't look any better, and the boy slowly became a lot quieter. That didn't worry him too much; Tierney had always been a bit broody. One night, some ordinary-looking fellows brought Tierney home, dead drunk with his feet a-dragging, as the song had it, at which Morgan was irrationally pleased.

The next morning, Morgan had the shift off, and was doing the bills in the kitchen. Late in the morning, Tierney came in, looking about uncertainly, blinking, puffy-eyed. Morgan leered at him mercilessly and sang, sotto voce, "Here I am, I'm drunk again."

"No more," Tierney croaked.

" 'No more,' is it? Well, I have said 'no more,' also, but I lied."

Morgan's humor passed unappreciated. Stoically, Tierney went through the motions of fixing himself some breakfast. Afterwards, he left for the shower.

After a time, he returned, dressed, looking more composed, if still a little shocked. He sat down across the table from Morgan and said, plainly, "A couple of nights ago, I had another visit."

For a minute, it didn't register with Morgan, but eventually it sunk in. "Leanne again?"

"Yes."

"What happened this time?"

"This time she took me to the city, showed me all around. If anything, it was even more real than the other times, except for one thing I noticed this time that I didn't before . . ."

"What's that?"

"This dream happened near morning, because I woke up before it, and it was just starting to get light outside. Between then and when I got up couldn't have been more than an hour. But in the dream I was there three days, and I remember every minute of it, except for when we were sleeping."

"In other words, inside the dream, you had a normal time scale of three days, and you slept, too? Sleeping in a dream?"

"Except those parts, everything was normal time flow."

"But only an hour in this world."

"Right. Exactly. The times don't match. It's not one-on-one."

Morgan asked, "In the other two, you were younger, but growing. What were you this time?"

"Just like now. I couldn't tell any difference at all."

"What did you do for three days?"

"Aw, c'mon!"

"Besides that."

"The same sort of things you'd do here, if you had three days off and a visitor you were very fond of. Nothing really out of the ordinary . . . at least, there.

I met some people, saw different things around the city."

"Tell me. What sort of people. Like us? And what sort of city? Is it ultramodern? Backward?"

"It's large, but more spread out. There aren't any tall buildings, more than three or four stories. Some wooden buildings, new and old, some masonry. There's no real center. It's like a lot of smaller towns grown together. I understand that it's very old, but it doesn't look like a relic, or anything saved in ruins. The people are just like here—they have jobs, live in apartments and some houses, only everything seems slowed down. Everybody had something to do, but they were very relaxed about it. At work, they seemed to be doing what they wanted to do. I met Leanne's . . . parents, although that's not quite it, either. There are four adults, and two are her actual parents; the other two are part of the household, very close, and to her the same. She has an older brother, Martin, although 'brother' isn't quite right either. I understood it there—it made sense, but it's hard to explain here . . ."

"Don't mind me. Go on, go on. It sounds nice. I can't get there myself, but I'd like to hear about it; it sounds as if you had a good time."

"You're not serious."

"Yes, I am, too. Now shut up and talk."

Tierney looked away for a minute, took a deep breath, and turned back, looking stern and resolute, but he was smiling in a secret way behind his eyes. "All right. They live in a house on a short street which is paved with cobblestones. The house is three stories, and has a line of tall, very slim trees growing beside it. They live on the third floor. Other folks live on the others. One is a city official, the other is a doctor.''

"Those others . . . did they have families?"

"The official had no other adults, but a lot of kids, from almost grown down to a couple of little ones. The doctor lived with two younger women, and one older. No kids."

"What do they do for a living?" Morgan asked, as if he thought he would hear something totally unexpected, like, "Her father is a meter-reader.''

"Leanne is still mostly a student, but when I say student, I don't mean it's like here. Sometimes she studies at home, under one or another of her parents. Other times, she goes to, like, different tutors. She has a lot of time. They call the teachers monitors. Part of the time she works in a bakery. Martin works on a canal boat, and also plays a sport. The grown people were as loose. I know what they do, but it's just detail. They don't buy their sense of identity from their work, which seems to make them a lot more whole, complete, and also makes the work better.''

"You stayed at her house?"

"It seemed natural to them. I felt odd, out of place, but they seemed to understand.''

"You slept with her, then.''

"Yeah. She had a small room in the back, facing a garden. The backs of the houses all face into sort of common ground. There was a small balcony, hardly big enough to stand on. They . . . didn't mind, or make any comment about it. It was like that everywhere; they weren't different. That's the way it's done, there."

"And it's clear, just like here?"

"Clearer. I feel like I actually went somewhere, and it scares me. I can't fit it with the world we live in here. I'm not crazy, but the strain between the two makes me worry."

Morgan laid his hand across the table, across the back of Tierney's hand. He felt a sudden relief. "No, don't worry about that. Crazy people are convinced, certain. If you think you're going bananas, you're saner than most, and if you think you're absolutely right, then you're mad as a hatter, well on the way to Pathology."

"And you don't mind hearing about this? I don't dare tell it anywhere else."

"Don't. As for me, I'd like to go there myself. Sign me up as a streetsweeper the next time you go. I could stand some slack."

The boy laughed out loud. "Right. I'll do that if it happens again!"

"Tell me about Leanne."

Now he hesitated, and then said, "She's about my age, more or less. A little more filled out, you know, than before, but the same person. She's blonde, her hair comes just past her shoulders. She's slim, almost delicate, a little shorter than me."

"Do they know where you come from?"

"That's the strangest part. They went to some trouble not to go on about it, but they know I'm from here, not another there-place. Apparently it's rare, but not impossible. In fact, Leanne's friend, Nyssa, was in the same situation, and was hosting a young fellow who seemed to be in the same situation I was, only he had more time there, and was working and going to school. Their way. I think he was there permanently. They all seemed to think that I would work out like he had. But they never said so directly. I mean, they are more . . . measured-out than us, but they're not dumb. They're subtle, they take time to do things right, they let things ripen. What do you think of all this?''

"I think it's the goddamnest thing I ever heard!" Morgan looked out the high kitchen windows at the filmy light, weak and watery, spilling in. After a while he said, "I guess we'd all like to have a better world. Somewhere, we went wrong here, and we all want another chance, only there isn't one here. Try to bring some of *that* back here with you, retain the good of it, and maybe in some unknown future, it could come true."

"When? Everything is on back-order, here."

"I don't know."

"When we left, we went on one of the canal boats out of the city, out into the grasslands. We walked out into the grass, same place she always meets me and leaves me, and she said that she thought it might take one more visit, and then if everything worked out, she'd come for me, for good."

"Jesus! When?"

"I don't know. There is some kind of Time problem. The two times don't fit except at certain places."

Morgan nodded. "Aha . . . now you have to be

careful. You go, in a dream, but your body stays here. Physics of this world.''

"Neither you nor I know what actually moves, do we?''

"Well, I don't stay up all night and watch you . . .''

"I'll try to bring something back with me.''

"Watch that. There might be some kind of energy problem, moving between places and leaving something behind. And by the way, why doesn't she come here?''

"Would you want to, if you lived *there?* Next question.''

Morgan looked at his watch, and started up. "I gotta go! I forgot what time it was. Work!'' He got all the way out of the kitchen, and then turned back. "Say, I'm serious. If it is real . . .''

Tierney laughed. "I know, I know. I'll tell them to come get you, too. What kind of girl do you want?''

Morgan thought for a moment, and then said, softly, "One I can indulge myself by being nice to.''

Morgan thought that he would hear about another of the Leanne dreams fairly soon, but as time now passed through its usual permutations without another word, he heard nothing, and hesitated to ask, fearing that he would create an obsession out of what might well be nothing more than the wish to escape of the prisoner. He couldn't see anything wrong with the latter; who wouldn't want a little escape? Just let them ask him, Morgan Maskelyne. Just once. No doubt about it.

Tierney went to more interviews, filled out more questionnaires, wrote more resumes. He came home laughing one day about a personnel officer who spoke at vast length about resumes and their importance, carefully pronouncing the word, "re-zoom." But other than that light moment, nothing changed. The sculpture of the girl's face slowly became more finished, more sharply focused, becoming sharper than in life, piercing; and then it vanished into Tierney's cabinet, with all the other marvelous things he'd made, the things nobody wanted, nor even wanted to talk about. Some days, Morgan would come home, to find Tierney sitting in the dark, staring at the video, awake but oblivious to whatever was being shown. Indeed, he seemed most of the time to take hardly any interest in what the subject was at all. To Morgan's routine questions he answered in monosyllables.

More than a little worried at last, Morgan checked in with the Ward Psychiatrist, who said a lot of words, but offered little encouragement.

"It's common, just common. Just stress. We put tremendous expectations on them throughout training, and when they finish and go out into the world, they can't all be chiefs. We need Indians. Just give him time, get him on the job somewhere. He'll get over it. Most of them do. Besides, he's legally an adult, so I can't treat him unless he volunteers for it, or is certified incompetent."

Morgan bit his lower lip, and said, "Well, that's the problem. He can't find anything but the rottenest sort of things. I see the stuff he does in his own time, and he's got abilities I wouldn't have dreamed of wanting to try to get, but there's nothing he can do that uses them.''

"He's signed up for the labor pool, isn't he?''

"Yes. The labor pool. All sorts of temporary stuff. Janitoring, street-cleaning. Road-mending. Standing around listening to losers.''

"He gets the labor pool stipend, doesn't he?''

The doctor shrugged. "He's got an income, hasn't he?''

"Income, yes. Regard for self, no. And if you don't have that for yourself, you can't get it from others. So everywhere he goes they tell him he's overqualified, for God's sake. Overqualified! He took the ELMATH Programming language, it was all the rage, they told him it was the wave of the future. Spent ten years on it. And so he finishes training and finds out that everywhere you go, they're using BIPOLAR, that old rag. And nobody is interested in putting on the time to reorient him.''

The doctor nodded, sagely, professionally. "Happens all the time.''

Morgan began to see that he really wasn't getting anywhere. It was just like trying to solve a recurring problem at work: they never gave answers—they just made excuses to do nothing. Anything to avoid putting your own ego on the line. He had learned to keep quiet, or at least to cover his butt. And as there, so here, the conversation was going in a circle. Morgan thanked the doctor, signed the billing with the receptionist, wincing at the charges. Oh, yes, the universal insurance paid for it, but that meant nothing.

They would just increase your premium. And for a lot of talk.

Morgan walked home, instead of riding the Magel. It was late. A slow, wet snow was falling, enormous damp flakes that melted instantly. He didn't pass many people along the way. An occasional truck, waddling through the streets, which were pocked with potholes like bomb craters. The trucks lurched and splashed iridescent waves over the streets. He smelled ripe garbage, diesel fumes, propane gas, pungent odors he couldn't identify, a waft from the rendering plant, blood and grease and decay, like bad breath with double exponents.

Morgan stopped off along the way at a beer hall where there was no merrymaking nor carousing, but silent patrons who kept to themselves and sipped at their brews. It was very late when he arrived at his block. The securityman at the door recognized him and mentioned, as he passed, "Your boy came in earlier."

Morgan nodded, and asked, "Didn't go back out?"

"No. Can't blame him, though—nothing going on on a night like this."

"Right you are."

Morgan took the lift to his floor, found his door, and went in. The front room was empty and the video was off. The kitchen light was on. He looked in, and saw that there was supper in the warmer. He looked at it blankly for a long time, but after a while, sat down and ate it stoically, with as little ceremony as possible. Then he poured himself another beer, a rare indulgence at home, and went back into the living room, to get sleepy before the viewer. Something different: he selected the Gymnastics channel and watched, mildly entranced, as the slender, muscular bodies of the supple, graceful girls went through their flowing, lovely motions. They needed no reason, no excuse. Half an hour of girls, and then half an hour of men and boys. Morgan went to sleep in the chair, while Milano Drasevich worked out on the horse.

Morgan had awakened at the same time for years, decades, and hardly needed a clock to wake him. Promptly at five, he woke up. He felt guilty about sleeping in the chair. He went into the kitchen to set some water on to boil. On the way to the shower, by force of habit, he looked into Tierney's room. There was no one there. The bed had been slept in, but there was nobody there.

Morgan went back into the living room, and checked the door he had locked last night. Still locked from the inside; the security bolts were still in place. No need checking the windows, they were all high up and too small to crawl through. He returned to Tierney's room, and, not touching anything, went carefully over it, looking closely at everything he could think of. He saw nothing out of order. The only thing he noticed that was odd was that the clothes Tierney had worn were still there, on the back of a chair, as he always left them. Morgan turned on the lights and looked again. There was nothing out of place. On the bed was a long, blonde hair, very pale, almost transparent. He wouldn't have

seen it if Tierney hadn't favored dark sheets. Beside
the hair was a small leaf, an odd sort of compound
leaf that looked ordinary enough to be from some
kind of weed. That was all. He listened. There was
no sound whatsoever, save the water, now boiling in
the kitchen. Morgan made himself a pot of instant
coffee, and then called the police. After that, he
called his workplace to tell them that he wouldn't be
in today.

By noon, a lieutenant Joe Horvath, of Missing Persons,
had arrived, with a forensic specialist in tow, and
while the specialist carefully went over the entire
apartment, Horvath took Morgan's statement, in which
he described everything he knew about events leading up to the disappearance. Morgan did not mention
the series of Leanne-dreams, or his interest in them.
Quite simply, he did not think Horvath would believe
him.

Horvath verified Morgan's statements with a small
polygraph, and then met with the specialist, who
produced the hair and the leaf. More properly, two
hairs, both long and pale blonde. Morgan's finger-
prints were the last ones on the doorlatch, and there
were no fresh prints on any of the windows. Horvath
said that it appeared to be an interesting and challeng-
ing case. But he told Morgan to go back to work. He
would be in touch. It was clear that the words weren't
much more than simple politenesses. And Horvath
added, pausing in the doorway, "Don't expect immediate results. I'm sorry, but we simply can't produce
them. We get a lot of cases similar to this, and many

of them aren't solved for months, years. Some, never. It's just the times we live in, I guess.''

Morgan nodded, absentmindedly; at least Horvath acted as if he were sincere. After the visit, Morgan allowed the numbness he had been holding off to settle on him with its full weight. Tierney was gone, without a trace. But where? Or, how could he have gotten out? Morgan checked the closet again. All Tierney's clothes, as far as he could tell, were where they should be. Nothing was missing. After a time, he left and went to work, automatically.

He allowed routine and fatigue to camouflage an emptiness which would not go away, but settled in and seemed to dig deeper, slowly, slow as the passage of the season. Morgan called Horvath a couple of times; in each case he had been told that Missing Persons Branch was doing all that they could, following out every possibility, as well as doing some intricate lab work that required considerable time. But that they in fact had nothing. Morgan walked in the streets, gray and damp with winter rain, sometimes glancing up at the leaden sky visible between the cornices of the buildings. He paid for an advertisement to run for a week on the local notices channel, but there was no answer, and in fact he had expected none.

One night, however, coming home from his second job, which he had kept out of habit, Morgan found Lieutenant Horvath waiting for him in the lobby of his apartment. They didn't say much on the way up, but inside, after Morgan had made coffee for the two of them, Horvath explained his visit.

"Damn, you keep beastly hours! I didn't know what time you got off, or if you still were working that second-shift job, so I waited."

Morgan made a polite sign with his free hand, and nodded slightly, as if suggesting that some things had no cure. Horvath continued, "I should start with the worst and tell you that we in fact have not turned up a single trace. The usual sources remain empty. Now a runaway tends to do certain things, statistically reliable, so to speak; this case hasn't followed any of them, our markers. We know that there was no foul play up until whatever time he disappeared—we covered that first. This is one of the more difficult ones."

Morgan stared at the cup for a time, and then asked, "What is there left that could be better?"

"We turned up a curiosity, which doesn't tie to anything. As a fact, it's so obvious that it looks like a deliberate message clue—sometimes they leave them like that. But what it says, or to whom it is addressed. . . ."

"Go on."

"Tierney had been the sole inhabitant of the bed: forensic. But on the bed they found those two hairs and a leaf."

"I saw them. I told you."

"Right. And that is why I haven't come sooner. Three *things*." Horvath said the last word with particular emphasis, making them sound like colossal artifacts of a vanished tribe, Easter Island statues, Haida totem poles. "We did all we could in our own lab, which is no slouch, and we couldn't believe it, so we sent them on to National Labs for complete teardown analysis. We have the report. What it says is this: the leaf is clearly a kind of sumac, genus *Rhus* is you're into taxonomy and systemics. It's a common weed-shrub or small tree all over the northern hemisphere. But this leaf isn't from any known variety."

Morgan shook his head, "Surely . . ."

"None. They have data on all plants down there, or what could reasonably be called most. They subjected it to every test, and those guys are good enough that they can identify local subspecies of plants. That leaf is a sumac: chemistry. But not of any known type, anywhere. Moreover, the pollutives common in varying degree to all plants, are extremely low in that sample, so we could not identify environmental factors at all. It is not from a pollution-free environment, but the contaminants are so low that it's no place we have data on."

Morgan didn't say anything. Horvath paused, and then continued, "The hair strands were even worse. Hair tell us a lot, internally and externally. Those two strands were cut, not broken, and they had been cut not long before we found them."

Morgan asked, "Who do they belong to?"

"A girl or woman, between eighteen and twenty-two, very fair-skinned, under medium height, slim but not petite."

"How could you know that?"

"Pattern of wear and kinking along the strand, other things. We traced every known associate of your son, and no one comes even close, moreover, no one can identify a girl of that decription. We have retraced almost all of his movements during the month previous, and no blonde girl there, either. No matter. I don't expect to find one.''

"Why?''

"It's like the leaf. Hair tells stories about where we live and how we live. Down at National Labs, they can take a sample and tell you where the person was within a ten-kilometer radius. That girl . . . didn't come from anywhere we can match the data to. Nowhere.''

Morgan said, slowly, "The sumac wasn't sumac; is the girl a girl?''

"Funny you'd say it that way; we did the same. The girl who grew the hair, as far as the lab can determine, is just an ordinary girl. Standard basic human being. But not from anywhere we can match. And the places we can match are highly improbable— just ridiculous—and spattered all over the place, too.''

"What sort of place might it be, say, typically?''

"Near salt water. Nearest industrial plant seems to be a cement kiln, but that's not real close. Higher selenium and zinc content than typical, but not alarmingly so. There were a couple of pollen grains, but although they are typical of extensive grasslands and open prairie, they don't match any better to a definite species. And that's why I'm here. We've run dry, and the chief suggested I stop by and ask if you knew any more, something we missed or forgot to ask, that might help.''

Morgan sat for a long time. "Do you still have the hairs and the leaf?''

"Oh, no. They were destroyed in testing. Nothing left. Just the report and the sheets of computer paper on the analysis. I have it on file."

Morgan stood up and put his cup in the sink. "I don't have anything. I had hoped your lab would be able to find something."

Horvath stood and offered his cup. "Well, in that case I'm sorry. I really am. This was one of those cases where nothing worked for us. We went at it harder than usual."

Morgan said, "I understand. Well, you'll still call?"

"Of course."

Morgan let Horvath out and returned to the living room, where he turned out the lights and sat for a long time in the darkness, remembering descriptions of a series of dreams. He went over it very carefully in his mind, so that he had it exactly as it had unfolded, in its own sequence, not the way he heard it. He didn't know how, and he couldn't explain it, but something inside his chest lightened its grip and he felt irrationally pleased. It made no logical sense, but then in its own terms, it made perfect sense. There was only one explanation. Somehow, Leanne had come for him, and they had managed to leave something behind. He didn't know why those things, why no message. But then, perhaps, as Horvath said, it was an excellent message. Morgan got up and went to bed, and went to sleep almost instantly.

He woke up early, remembering an odd, very clear dream he had had. He had been in a grassy field, the grass golden with early autumn. Not far away there was a line of low, widespreading trees that seemed to conceal a watercourse, and out of the trees a girl had come walking. It had been then that he noticed himself. He seemed a lot younger—Morgan thought perhaps fourteen or fifteen. The girl wore a loose blue dress that came to her knees, and called herself Nory, or Norrie. It was a little awkward. After they had introduced themselves, he asked her where they were. She had said that he couldn't ask yet, but if he wanted she could come back when (something) changed again. It was a word he didn't recognize and couldn't remember. Morgan had looked at the girl, who was graceful rather than pretty, with a loose, mobile face that registered emotions well. She had soft brown hair which fell in artless curls along her shoulders. And he told her that he would like very much to come back. He had watched her turn and walk back into the trees, and disappear, and he looked around him at the world. Blue sky, golden sunlight, a cool breeze ruffling the grass and stirring the trees along the watercourse. Yes. Here, but not here. Awake, in his own bed in the gray morning, he wondered where, how, what time. And then he said to himself silently, *don't question it*. He wasn't completely convinced; but all the same, he remembered the scene deliberately, and very secretly hoped that he might meet Nory, or Norrie, again. And Tierney.

THE CONVERSATION

I have to admit that the question I personally find most aggravating of all is the one that goes, "And what is the story X about?" I usually answer that it is about sex and evolution. Sometimes I say sex and revolution. It's all the same, as an answer which suits the question. I mean, I find it distressing that anybody imagines that a story, however long or short, can be compressed into a single one-liner which competes well with other buzz-word conversation.

However that is, here is one story in which I went to extremes to prevent condensation by any manner. If I said what it was about, I would be longer in that telling than in the story itself.

I always try stories out first. One of my readers told me it didn't sound very "science-fictiony." But there is a "gotcha" in this story, which makes it so, and when I had hinted enough, this person said, "Oh, yeah, I see, oh, God. . . ." Science Fiction is speculation, right? I mean, it's still okay to ask questions, isn't it? So let Mila Vekshin and Constantin Forgesi speak for themselves. They do so better than I can say for them.

It was evening in Jelusidac, and the violet shadows
of the buildings to the west had already swept across
the expanses of Vladny Prospekt, the plaza which
was the center of the Capital's system of radiating
streets. Equally important, it was the frame which
displayed for the visitor and citizen alike its remarkable railroad terminal, which had been built in the
ground plan of an equilateral triangle, presumably the
only one such in the entire world. One face fronted
the plaza, while the sides behind accommodated tracks,
the left one on an upper level, the right on a lower.
The building itself was of a tan stucco with dark
woodwork, and on the plaza side, two-story windows
of many panes overlooked Vladny Prospekt. The roof
was of a burnt-orange tile familiar to the region.
Three small office suites occupied flat-roofed dor-
mers emerging from the roof, one to each side, and
the building culminated in a tower which ended in an
observation cupola, rather like an aircraft control
tower, with a circular plan and outward-canted
windows.

An observer who happened to be in one of the
government offices opposite the terminal could easily
see at this time of day how the shadows rose like a
tide across the Prospekt, engulfing the monument to
the veterans of the Battle of Budgorno Forest, engulfing the terminal until only the tile roof and the central
tower were left glowing in the rosy golden evening
light, and finally painting the retaining wall on the
left side of the terminal wings a warm coppery color.

The clock on the face of the tower shaft noted that it was now five-thirty.

If this observer (and there was likely none, the government offices being closed long ago, being government offices) had been especially keen-sighted, or had a small telescope, he could have observed the shifts change in the cupola. And after a reasonable delay, he could have observed a tall, sturdy woman emerge from the terminal main doors and walk briskly, with a loose, relaxed stride, some distance out onto the Prospekt, to stand waiting at the tram stop with others. From this distance, he would have seen a woman not greatly different from many others which could be seen this time of day: A kerchief about her hair, a pale raincoat with a belt, carrying a net bag and a newspaper, and wearing black, sturdy, sensible shoes. She adjusted her scarf and pulled her collar fractionally tighter against the evening's chill (it was winter). She stood erect and looked over the evening crowds with animation and interest, and when the proper tram pulled into the siding, boarded without delay. The tram bore the nameboard of Soblaznaya, a district on the southwestern side of the city.

Constantin pushed his typewriter back a bit, leaned back, and squinted critically at the pages he had written, reading rapidly. He finished, and nodded to himself in satisfaction. Yes. That was a proper beginning.

Constantin Forgesi was a writer, but you may never have heard of him. Although he did have something of an international following, he was by no means famous, and never had to conceal his identity. Often featured in magazines specializing in fantasy, he was more properly a surrealist who wrote careful and intricate distortions of selected realities which occasionally walked along the very borders of madness. Some well-disposed critics had compared him with such as Borges, Gogol, Céline, Nabokov and Kafka. Others, no less cogently, had called him a charlatan, an idiot, and a congenital cretin.

However that went, it can be readily understood that Constantin did not make very much money, and so lived modestly and alone in an apartment in the Prunomonte section of Libreville. He had a few close friends, most notably Anna M, the existential-ist poet (who had been, in an earlier day, a lover), and Ramon O., who had once been a great revolu-tionary in his day but who now made a living paint-ing realist covers for popular editions of novels and anthologies, as well as similar covers for the jack-ets of phonograph records.

What Constantin intended to accomplish in this story (to be called "The Endurance of Mila Veksin") was to depict a person who successfully resisted the sapping erosions of modern life—erosions, for symbolic purposes, examined in the context of slightly past time, in a preposterous fictional slavonic coun-try otherwise unspecified and unidentifiable. His de-vice would be the perception of the effects of the introduction of some device or methodology which would not in itself be new, but would only be so in that country.

Constantin thought that it should work well; after all, he could readily identify with such an idea, himself. He could not rid himself of the notion, however well-denied by others, that a certain quality of life was declining in exact proportion to the arrival of the long-forecast age of marvels. He himself had, during his lifetime, observed the introduction of many new things, discoveries, technologies. And had, in turn, observed that people did not seem to be liberated by these creations, but instead gave up and became dependent on them. His common-sense skepticism told him that much of this was probably no more than a case of longing for the good old days. Such things were unavoidable. And yet, even allowing a fudge factor for such thinking, a hard core remained which would not go away and lie quietly.

From the first, he had had trouble with the story. Nothing had jelled, and his first drafts had quickly run off into an endless maze of details, losing the direct narrative thrust that every story, however slight, needs to have to come off properly. And Mila Vekshin proved to be, far from being the simple girl he imagined her to be, a most difficult character. At first, Constantin could not make her "live" at all. Then, when he succeeded, she would not respond to the usual controls a writer had at his disposal, the events he could throw at her. She survived them all with stolid persistence. She had none of the features of contemporary heroines, and in the world he had put her in, little chance to develop them.

This was important, for "bringing a character to life" was one of the most difficult parts of all writing. Indeed, many successful stories were sold and prospered which failed in this, being content with symbolic images and stereotypes. The most important part of the process was that the character had to have considerable leeway, a free will, as it were, and yet remain controllable.

But Constantin kept after it, and soon a pattern began to emerge, and Mila woke up and came to life. She began to take on dimension and depth. At that point, Constantin sent the unfinished manuscript to Ramon, to see if he could "see" her. He could, and did. In less than a week, Ramon promptly sent the manuscript back, accompanied by a set of careful, if sparse, pencil drawings which depicted Mila in various circumstances: Waiting for the tram to Soblaznaya; at work in the tower; cooking in her flat; one nude illustration, drying her hair after a bath (although not fat or even plump, she did have a sturdy, powerful body that suggested a certain classicism). In all of these, she seemed to possess, in her face, and most especially in the eyes, an expression of intense, concentrated regard, as if she could, simply by trying hard enough, unravel the riddles. It was a face that could be transported by love, or wrenched with sadness and pain, but it would never stay so long. This worried Constantin a bit. Mila was showing her independence as a character, her "life," too soon.

*   *   *

Mila Vekshin had come from the backward province of Dubnovo, an altogether unremarkable girl of the country who had met and married a dashing but dissolute officer of the Armored Corps, Igor Vekshin. After his posting to the Capital, and after a series of scandals, Igor had abandoned his bride, making certain financial arrangements. Shortly thereafter, his apparently continued misconduct had resulted in his being broken to the ranks, and sent to the Eastern Steppe. The money, never great, faded, sputtered, and vanished.

These events, not atypical, served to put some fire in Mila's previously uneventful life. She had, with country simplicity, drawn upon the one source she could depend upon—herself. And as usual in such cases, had discovered resources she hadn't known existed. On the strength of Igor's fading connections, she secured for herself a position in the Ministry of Railroad Communications, and leased a flat in the Soblaznaya district. Moreover, she did so well that she was promptly promoted. Her assumption of the role had been so complete that to this day at work she was referred to, with some deference, as "Madame Vekshin." She wore the dark maroon skirt and jacket of the Civil Service as though she had been born to it. And with her habit of losing herself and whatever daunted her, or worried her, in her work of scheduling trains and tracking down errant shipments, she soon earned their genuine respect. Mila had grown into the robust figure of the girls of her part of the country, so she would never be one of the svelte and fashionable girls of the Capital. She increased her

distance by wearing spectacles and combing her luxuriant hair up in a severe bun.

Within herself, she regarded what she had accom-
plished as the wildest sort of magic act, and occasionally paused to marvel at it. But not too much. For she
instinctively knew that if one wondered overly at
one's good fortune, it could tremble, waver, and
vanish overnight.

Only at home, in the small flat above a small
machine shop, at night, safely alone, did she relax
part of her vigilance. And although in school she had
been competent but not notable, she now diligently
wrote down, in a commonplace copybook, her
observations, which were the only anchors in the new
reality she found herself in. And although she had
not lived with Igor long, she had learned, curiously,
a soldierlike sense of the proper virtues necessary,
from him. They were simple: *Live simply. Don't
volunteer. Do solid work and don't make a fuss
about it—if they don't notice, all the better. Keep
quiet and stay invisible—never let the Commandant
know your name. The only ones he knows are trouble-
makers and rivals. Take your pleasures sparingly,
for rarity gives value. And savor them, for in fact
they are few.* Igor's main vice had been that he had
steadfastly refused to listen to his own excellent
advice.

Constantin had wanted to set up a situation in
which Mila would be drawn by her nature into an
inescapable conflict of motivations, and these motivations had to be given or implied early on in the

story. But she seemed cold, ruthless, and even a little predatory. And damned alert: he knew that he'd have to be careful. Mila was clearly a survivor, and as crafty and alert as a bull Marmont.

Anna dropped by to see how things were going. Constantin showed her the story, so far, and told her some of what he had in mind. After she had read what was there, she commented, "Yes, she does seem a little cold now; but after all, that is reasonable in the circumstances you have her in—a backward girl in a backward country in a backwater of time. And she was abandoned by a rascal."

Constantin added, somewhat lamely, "Well, Igor respected her and confided secrets to her. I imagine that he married her for her virtues. After all, he could find vices well enough on his own."

Anna thought for a moment, stroking her fingers through her faded brown-gold hair. Then she suggested, "You could always have her loosely engaged with a lover. Perhaps two, one on the side, so to speak."

"Well, I don't want to make her out to be a hussy. That would be completely out of character."

"No, no, not a tart! Just someone who has a definite idea of who she is, and of some little pleasures she might have. Say, one more formal, a suitor who wants her to divorce Igor . . ."

"A difficult process requiring ecclesiastical permission in that country . . ."

"But in those circumstances, eventually allowable. And then she'd have a hopeless character who was

ever so good to her. Try that one. It's by no means
rare."

"I'll think about it. But that's tricky, you know."

Mila stepped down from the tram and waited for it to
pass on before crossing the street. The workday was
over and she was back in her own part of the city.
The noises and odors were familiar and reassuring. A
dim streetlight illuminated the corner, while the tram
rattled off westward on its narrow-gauge rails and its
overhead electric lines hissed and sparked. Those
faded, to be replaced by the soft watery muttering of
the River Syrma, hardly more than a few meters back
toward the city, tumbling down through a narrow
little cut which ran parallel to the street she lived on.
The odor of leaves and water.

Number two Plezskoch Street, second on the right,
the upstairs part of a plain wooden building. The
small machine shop which took up the first floor was
always closed at night. And the few times Mila had
seen it open, it had been quiet. Whatever they did
there seemed to make little noise. She walked along
the edge of the cobblestoned street until she came to
the end of the shop, and then turned in underneath
the overgrown privets, which had grown up from a
hedge and become trees shading the south of the
building. She unlatched the gate, and walked along a
narrow walkway to the back, where a long wooden
stair led up to the second floor.

Once inside, Mila wasted no time. Leaving her
shoes by the door, she negotiated the L-shaped living
room and went around to her left, to her bedroom,

where she carefully took off her uniform and hung it up. Then she wrapped herself in a loose dressing-gown. While supper was cooking, she attended to the flat, straightening things, checking the mail, and laying out things for the next day. Sometimes she hummed parts of songs she had heard; parts folksongs and rondelays from Dubnovo Province, cabaret airs she had heard in passing in the city, mournful love songs. She did not hurry, but managed to finish about the time supper was ready.

After supper, she cleaned up the kitchen, a narrow little cramped room at the south end of the flat, and, satisfied that everything was ready for the next day, bolted the door, and went back, through the bedroom to the bathroom, where she drew a tub of hot water, which she sank into gingerly, at last stretching out and relaxing. She unbound her hair and let it fall in loose curls into the water, some of it trailing along her shoulders, and let her mind go perfectly blank. Time no longer mattered. Here, now, was where she really sorted things out, made decisions.

Mila thought, semi-disconnectedly, letting it drift where it would: *discipline, attention to details, that's what makes it work. Never let go. Like sailing a boat. All that I learned from Igor, that strange devil. And other things, too.* She smiled, faintly, and made an involuntary, luxurious movement with her hips, tensing her abdomen. *And it works, too. Why ever did he fail? Wicked man, he had a darkness in him, and it swallowed him up. He did things to me, with me, that I couldn't have imagined, wouldn't have dared, but when he left it was probably for the best*

*because I feared him. That's settled. And now I'm
here in the great wicked Capital, Jelusidac, and I
can't go back to Dubnovo. And no sooner do I get
settled in good, here, than they bring up this new
thing, a computer. The latest thing. Most modern.
Contemporary. A marvel. And that fat Subdirector
Masinen, gabbling fool, an Estoty no less, and he
wants me to tell him what I think of it. They say it
will keep all our schedules, register the ladings, even
run the switches and the signals. And no doubt heal
the sick, raise the dead, and make all the girls talk
out of their heads.* She added the last on,
irreverently. *And there's something wrong with that
modern thing, but I can't find it. But I know it's
there.*

Constantin, at his next meeting with Anna, con-
fessed to a certain bafflement. "I tried what you
suggested, but it wouldn't fit. I could have forced it,
you know, had someone thrown gravel on her porch,
or whistle from the garden, or similar nonsense, but
it felt wrong and I'm sure the reader would notice
the discontinuity."

Anna took up the manuscript and read through
what Constantin had so far. After a moment, she
looked up and nodded, briskly. "I see that, too.
She's damn difficult. You can make her do things,
but only at the risk of disturbing the flow of the story
itself."

"You don't think she's too cold? Too calculating?"

"Oh, no. Not that at all. Something entirely else."

Constantin was silent for a long time. Then he

said, "Actually, she's not cold at all. She's extremely erotic, intensely. I can feel it. But it's as if somehow she's, ah . . . partitioned it off some way, and she has me following her rules."

Anna nodded, agreeing. "And if you're Mila, you don't lose your head. Period. That's clear. I like her."

"What do you mean, you 'like her'?"

"Sometimes, certain men have a toughness that other men know is real, and admire. Not the false posturing, but the real thing, which is nearly invisible. Women have a toughness, too. But the two aren't the same. So Mila is Woman-Tough, do you follow me? And women like that aren't all that common, in the same way. So just give her a little time; don't rush her. If you rush her, she'll just dig in and defy you."

Constantin laughed, "It's supposed to be a short story, not a novel!"

"Yes, I understand. But what makes a story good is not its length in words, but its expansiveness, the way it puts down roots outside and beyond itself. en you start to see true things in it that you didn't put there. It's a window, not a closed box!"

"Of course I put them there."

Anna said, with a sage sidelong glance, "You put them there, but you don't know their power."

Mila had turned out the lights and gone to bed. Before she went to sleep, she habitually imagined herself as a young girl, standing barefoot in the sandy mud of Spring in Dubnovo, shooing the birds out of the Staghorn Tree, a great overgrown knotty thing by the path to the granary. She had been tall for her age, even then, and had filled out early. But nobody had seemed to notice, because she had been proportioned well. It helped her to remember these things; she was always careful to consider who she was, who she had been, who she was becoming. You could only do so much. Even Igor had said so much: *Take your portion and don't ask for seconds.*

In the dark, the room lit only by the weak glow from the corner streetlamp, she heard the gate-latch trip, and then, soft, unhurried steps on the stairs. A pattern of steps she knew well. After a moment had passed, there was a low knocking at the door. She listened, and then rolled over, away from the bedroom door. No. Not tonight.

The knock repeated. She could let it go. She knew who it was. Finally she rolled back, sleepily and slightly irritated, and got up, pulling her dressing gown around her. When she went to the door of the flat, she did not turn the lights on. She said, through the closed door, "Go away. It's too late. I have to get up and go to work tomorrow morning. Early." Somehow, it didn't sound convincing, even to her. She added, "I mean it."

A voice answered, "Very well. At least let me kiss you good night."

"No."

"Mila . . ."

"No, Afanasy. Go home."

"Ludmila . . ." Nobody ever called her by her full name, even Igor. Except Afanasy. She unlocked

the door and opened it a crack, with a curious duality
in her heart, one part a sinking feeling of bottomless
doom, and another, equally important, a sudden rush
of breathless excitement. She leaned out into the chill
night air, now becoming foggy. She saw the tall
shape in the dark, slender, and she found his face,
pressed her cheeks against his, on each side, touched
her mouth to his, primly. She stepped back and said,
"And now, good night."

She smelled the night on him, outsideness. He had
probably walked all the way out here. There was a
hint of plum brandy about his mouth, faintly, and
when he touched her arm, she let him stay a moment
longer. She stepped back a little, but did not shut the
door, and Afanasy stepped through, but not boldly.
Tentatively, shyly. He set his books down and shut
the door. Afanasy was a sometimes-student at the
University. He kissed her again, lightly, not forcing
her, and she felt herself relaxing, melting. He opened
her gown gently, almost absentmindedly, and with
his fingertips traced an imaginary line down the center of her body, from the hollow of her throat, between her breasts, along the soft curve of her belly.
He touched her hair, parted the dense, curly strands
and touched her there. His fingertips were cold, but
that was insignificant. It was so easy, so gentle; she
could stop it anytime. Her legs felt weak. She said,
her voice unsteady and hoarse, "Please go . . ."

"No."

"No," she agreed, and pulled him to her, fiercely,
somehow managing to shut and bolt the door. Then
she gave herself completely to the flow of it, sud-

denly throwing down and forgetting all the careful outlines of her life, all of them. She led Afanasy around the sofa into the small bedroom, where she helped him pull his clothing off, and then drew his outside-cool body to her, into her, slim and wiry as a snake and at the center of that coolness and the night there was something wet and hot and sudden that made her breath catch in her throat for an impossible endless moment, which didn't end so much as it faded into a longer time in which they remained engaged, still moving, reaching for the perfect moment. And much later she finally persuaded him to leave because she was strict on that—she would never allow Afanasy to stay there.

She heard him stumble a little at the foot of the stairs, outside, as befuddled as she was, and she laughed to herself, a rich, warm laugh, as she wrapped the covers around herself, her bare body, to go to sleep, and as she sank into it, she whispered fiercely to herself *Loose woman that you are, Ludmila, a most shameless tart!* But she was smiling, and her heart felt like some impossible flower expanding out into the familiar outlines of the room, dimly lit by the corner streetlamp.

When she arrived at work the next morning, she followed her routine exactly: at the coffee shop on the first floor of the Terminal she purchased a nut-covered sweet roll which they called *karabashka* here, but which she knew in her home dialect as a *lezhyonka*. Then she climbed the the spiral stairs to the top of the tower. At the top, she wasn't breathing hard, but she

did feel lightheaded, and she smiled at the recollection of the night before, which was probably the
cause of it. *What a peculiar activity,* she thought; *it
makes you weak and strong at the same time.* She felt
light, airy, full of meaning and purpose.

At her desk, she stopped to consider the memo-
randa left there by the night shifts, and slyly glanced
out the windows onto the morning of the city,
daydreaming. Momentarily seduced, she leafed through
the memos aimlessly, deferring them all for a moment.
They were rare enough. One note caught her eye, as
she skimmed past it, and she stopped, woke up, and
looked more closely. It said: "Masinen. 9:00." That
was his curt and tactless way of telling her to come to
his office. Sometimes he would call up on the telephone and say, recognizing her voice, "Pad and
pencil," which meant he had a list of things to go
over. Impossible! Absurd, he was. Did not Masinen
understand that manners were the only thing that held
the world together? Nothing else, not armies in the
night, not glowering dictators, not processions! Obviously not. But, she reflected, what could one expect
from an estoty. She understood that he was from
Wafna, on the northwest coast, with its monotonous
flatlands and fens. Masinen was a fussy little bald
man, round as an egg, with porcelain-blue eyes which
were blank as agates and revealed little except the
most obvious and reptillian emotions. And Wafna!
Impossible city, too! She had been there, once, on
business for the Ministry. On the city gates they had
even had a latinate motto, 'Quid Facisti Sors Tur-
pissima.' *What hast thou done o infamous fate.* Indeed!

Mila ranked Masinen somewhere along with, say, shortages of basic household items, or noxious fumes from the shunting-yards south of the tower, as things she had to endure in this life.

At 9:00, she left her work in the tower cupola and went back down the spiral to the office levels far down the echoing shaft. There was a circular landing there, and three suites, with frosted glass doors, and names on them: Borenko, Construction. Avvakum, Accounting. Masinen, Administration. She went in without knocking. The offices were long, ending in pleasant windows facing out over the triangular roof sections of the terminal. Masinen's looked over Vladny Prospekt, now a luminous pool filled with bright morning light. Masinen sat back in his chair by the window, and on the other side of the window was a visitor. He motioned for her to come to them. Masinen introduced the visitor as a Citizen Maksim of the United Provinces. And after introducing her, he explained, "Citizen Maksim is the commercial factor who will oversee the installation of the new control system."

Mila said, quietly, "Then it has definitely been decided to go ahead with it?"

"Of course. This issue has been one of paramount importance for the Narodny Sobor. It was deliberated, so I am told, at the highest levels of the Praesidium."

Mila understood through the pompous screen of formula-words well enough and needed no further explanations. *No discussion. Do it.* She said, carefully, "How may I be of service?"

Masinen indicated to Maksim that he should speak,

if he would. Maksim began hesitantly, obviously speaking a language foreign to him, but on the whole, not doing badly. Maksim was a youngish man of indeterminate age, thin and sandy-haired, nervous, who seemed to have the air of being a somebody, somewhere else. Here, he was scared half to death. He said, "Director Masinen has spoken highly of you and has told me that you are most familiar with the control routines involved and how the different sections are orchestrated (Mila mentally corrected the word to read 'coordinated'). I would be honored to work with you on this project." He finished, proud of his speech, which had been, despite the odd, flattened accent, rather well-done.

Mila asked, "What would we be doing?"

Maksim indicated two fingers. "One, to install the components and test them without disrupting current operations, and two, to start it up with as little . . . ah, stormishness . . .?"

Mila suggested, "Turbulence?"

"Yes, turbulence, thank you." He looked as if he were about to call her by name, but he wasn't quite sure enough of the proper forms to try. He smiled, weakly. "In replacing an existent system, one has to proceed carefully."

Mila listened, but another part of her was questioning and alert. There was definitely something here, unseen, but implied, that she must not miss. But what was it? Masinen? Not so. He was already bored, having turned the problem over to her. Not Masinen. He was clearly a functionary who had done his bit and now he could shrug and say, "It wasn't *my* job."

So it had to be Maksim—or what he was saying. There was something not right here, but she couldn't quite see it. It was just out of reach. She asked, "When do we start?"

"Immediately. Today, if you are ready."

Mila nodded her agreement. "We can begin with the layout of the Central Sector, and the ways and times in which the Provincial Branches feed into it."

Maksim was pleased to meet such a knowledgeable and cooperative member of the staff. "Here?"

"No, upstairs, in the cupola. It's all up there."

Constantin looked closely at the section he had just finished and shook his head, more than a little uncertain. He read through it again, squinting owlishly at the text. There was no doubt that it ran with the oily smooth inevitability of reality, but nonetheless, Mila mulishly refused to act as he wanted her to. To some extent, this was in part a desirable trait in well-done characters, after they "came to life," so to speak—they would of a natural course be somewhat disobedient and unruly. But Mila Vekshin. His control of her actions seemed sporadic and weak, and he began, regretfully, to consider putting the story aside for a while. Perhaps even scrubbing it. After all, what was the purpose of a story, anyway? To entertain people, illuminate them, maybe instruct them . . . Certainly not to provide Mila Vekshin with a world to inhabit.

He decided to step out for a bit, walk down to a nearby cafe, and have an apéritif. Constantin put on his coat, scarf, and flat-topped cap, locked up his apartment, and made his way down the Moorish exterior stairway, an echoing concrete tube with oval openings to the outside. Very arty, but that was why he liked these apartments so much. Ventebrulanto Corto. He walked down his street, the Verda Strato, to the cafe, O Polva Tamburo, where he ordered a glass of Dormi-Eble-Sonği, and settled back near the front window to enjoy it. The first one seemed to clear away some of his uncertainties, so he ordered another, this one with a tiny cup of espresso. Constantin looked through the window, store-front plate glass, frosted over with condensation, to the blurred forms outside, some of them rather recognizable as trees and buildings. The trees were bare with winter and damp-black from the drizzle. There were other forms visible which did not resolve so readily. People, most likely. You could tell because they moved around, even though their forms were indistinct. Yes, they were people; he was sure of it. Knowing that reassured him and satisfied his natural urge to perceive clearly-defined forms. He knew what those shapes were, therefore it was sufficient. The blurred shapes moved back and forth across his field of vision through the sweat-blurred pane, intent on their own errands and missions, which Constantin felt certain were mostly trivial.

The second apéritif was somewhat stronger than he recalled the first being, and Constantin slowly settled inside himself, like a sack of dry rice adjusting to its neighbors in a warehouse. A slow, glacial, imperceptible procedure, but inevitable. And as he settled, he imagined Mila, features of her which he knew as well as he knew any person, any woman. Yes, as well as Anna. Mila: her broad, slavonic face, sturdy, square shoulders (which were nicely rounded and dimpled when bare), full, well-developed breasts. Her pale skin, cool and smooth. Her long fingers. Yes. She had a problem there: her hands were immense for a woman, and she always had difficulty purchasing gloves for ladies in the shops of Jelusidac. . . .

. . . . He next noted that someone was shaking his shoulder. It was the barman with his apron, striped shirt, and broom. He looked at Constantin, saw that he was back in this world, and said, " 'Ey, civit'ano! Time to go home, ehe?"

Constantin shook his head slightly to clear some of the cobwebs away. He looked at the barman in turn, as if he were some emissary from the Crab Nebula. No, further: the Andromeda Galaxy. Even that wasn't far enough. M87 in the Virgo Cluster might do the trick: he looked strange. But he said, "Yes, yes, of course."

Constantin walked out into the soft gray-blue drizzle twilight, the background tone promising a cold, damp night. Maybe more rain. He pulled his scarf a little tighter, and snugged his brown cap down closer to his ears. He did not return up his own street, but turned off onto the Strato do Flava Hundo, which was where Anna now lived, renting a loft over a guitar shop.

But when he passed by the shop, there were no lights in the loft, and so he continued on his way home, deep in thought, and for the first time, a little wary. *I mean, it's not like she's flesh and blood, a real woman, someone I could meet on the sly. She's nothing but a figment of my imagination. I could burn the manuscript, and that would be that, eh? Tout à toi, Madame Vekshin!* He thought that, and stepped forward, briskly, full of resolve, but all the same there was a small shadow in his mind which all the bravado in the world would not quiet.

When Constantin returned to his apartment, he hung his coat up and placed his cap on a peg in the wall, and fixed supper in his tiny kitchen (There was hardly enough room to turn around), and ate with the stolid determination of an ironworker, still half angry and full of dire will. But afterwards, when he had put up the dishes, brewed himself a pot of coffee, and was standing over his writing-table like an avenging angel, with the manuscript actually in his hand (There was a fifty-gallon drum at the foot of the landing outside, which served as a garbage can. He could burn it there), then his second-thoughts took on more form and substance. The pages glared at him whitely, full of imprecations, threats, horrid promises. He couldn't quite understand the message, but he was certain that he was receiving one; one didn't become a surrealist writer by ignoring hints, however bizarre.

Now Constantin sat down, trying to reason it out. *Mila is just a character in a story; destroy the manuscript and that's the end of it, right?*

Wrong. The story and the character is in my head, and . . . right. Constantin, being a surrealist,

could appreciate the irony. For years he had pro-
pounded the theory that you had to bring a character to life, and that a truly living character would
make some moves purely on initiative. It sounded
like mumbojumbo, but it worked. Equally important
was his other theory, which held that the story was
an indefinable entity which actually occurred in the
reader's mind, not on the paper. What was on
paper was only a set of keys, instructions to the
memory, which would in turn flesh out the story and
truly bring it to life. What went on, on the printed or
typed page was relatively unimportant, so long as it
made the story-in-the-mind take place. *A prisoner
of my own success, a prisoner of my own device.*
He sat down at the typewriter, abruptly. *I could
have her run over by a tram. But then, I wouldn't
have a story. Absurdity is only valuable when the
focus of the story is the absurdity itself. So Mila is
hostage to me, but now so am I to her. No less. I
can only escape her by finishing the story, by leading her through to the conclusion and its implications of continuity that were implicit in it from the
first word. "It was evening in Jelusidac." Indeed.*
That was also one of his pet theories, and he
grimaced at it. It was bitter, now. *Very well.* He
began typing, again.

Mila had been explaining a minor procedural point to
Maksim, when she suddenly felt a sense of danger so
acute that it made her faint and lightheaded. She
looked about sharply, glancing out the windows of
the observation cupola, and among the clerks and

displays within; but there was nothing there. Nonetheless, the world felt unreal and wavering. She excused herself for a moment, left the cupola, and hurriedly went downstairs to the ladies' lavatory, where there was a plain couch for those difficult days. The feeling persisted. She lay down and tried to feel where in herself the sensation was coming from. Pregnant? Impossible. And it was also the wrong time of the month for peculiar feelings. At any rate, she had been taking a prescription drug to regularize her menstrual cycle and prevent conception, and that had taken care of most of that, at least the worst of it. *It isn't that.* She concentrated, exerting the same sensation of will and determination she had used after Igor had abandoned her and things had seemed so bad. *Survive!* She began to feel better, and she let herself become angry, and that helped, too. The feeling of unreality passed, and things seemed to return to normal. She shook her head, as she sat up on the couch. *Chyortu Zhyopa!* An oath from her provincial and agricultural childhood escaped her with a hiss of breath, while she moved her mouth, forming the words but not daring to say them aloud.

She felt better, now, but the feeling persisted that she had been in deadly peril, narrowly escaped, something unimaginable and total. Something worse than death. What?

Mila retained from her country background an explicit trust in her senses, even when their messages were incomprehensible. She had felt as if she had been in danger, so then so had she been; it was as simple as that. But what precisely it might have

been, she might never know. She removed a small
notepad from an inside pocket of her jacket, and
there she made a short note, a reminder. This was
something worth noting.

She returned to the cupola, where Maksim was waiting.
He said, "Are you feeling quite well? You seemed
alarmed."

"It was nothing, thank you. Perhaps I stayed up
too late last night; I had some work at home. But
thank you. Now, observe this connection which runs
from Wafna, through Jelusidac, and to here, at
Kapustingrad. It's like the trunk of a tree . . ." And
so Mila continued her descriptions to Maksim, as if
nothing had happened.

Mila took lunch, as was her custom, in the cafete-
ria on the first level of the terminal, in a section
reserved for employees of the Ministry. Maksim had
excused himself, explaining that he was required to
attend a luncheon with other officials.

After lunch, Maksim soon returned, and now they
went through the various reporting procedures, many
of which were complex and required various forms of
authentication and documentation. It was dry, hard
stuff, but necessary—the system wouldn't function
without it, or something like it; and on those points
they were agreed.

Toward evening, some clouds began drifting in
from the west, obscuring the sunset and bringing an
early darkness. A melancholy steam whistle from the
marshalling yards south of the terminal signaled the
end of the workday, and Mila went to the coat rack

to retrieve her raincoat, kerchief and scarf. By the stairwell rail, Maksim asked her, "Would you be free for dinner tonight? I must tell you that I was impressed with your grasp of this system as a system; in my work I meet very few people, I assure you, who are capable of appreciating that."

"Thank you, but please, not tonight. I am a bit tired—I fear I would be poor company. And besides, I would want to get my clothes in order for such an event; I shouldn't want to have dinner with a foreign official dressed up like some matron of the actuarial department." But she smiled when she said it.

"Some other time, then. May I insist?"

"Certainly. I would like that. Perhaps in a day or so."

Maksim made a polite gesture, and turned to watch the heavy tank engines puffing up and down the rails in the yards.

Mila was a creature of routine, because she sensed that in some situations routines were all that stood between yourself and chaos. But by the same coin, you had to allow some time to have a little joy, too. A little foolishness. And time to consider. Tonight, after her bath, wrapped in her dressing gown, she removed her copybook from its drawer, and set it on the table, open. She reflected for a moment, chewing on the end of the pen. Then she wrote:

A number of odd things have happened lately. They are simple in themselves, but together they add up to a whole that seems not to make sense.

In fact, they make me question what I thought
was right and proper about the whole past.

She stopped, read it over, and nodded to herself.
Below that, she listed a number of things she had
noticed in brief, concise descriptions. These included
Maksim and his project, but there were other things
as well, small things which fit into the whole, as she
saw it. She was sure she had missed some things, but
for now, this list would have to do. She considered
this list for a time, and then wrote:

You can always find real things by the eddies
and traces they leave in their passage: trains,
streetcars, trams. People who have real power.
Whatever it is that makes the wind blow.

That one surprised her. It opened up a whole new
range of possibilities. She put a small star by the
passage, so she could remember to come back to it.
But there was something else. This she wrote, just
below:

Little truths fit together like a puzzle, but
smoothly, to form bigger and bigger truths. The
false things don't fit, no matter how good they
sound. But that's the problem. Most people want
things to sound good, and to hell with the fit—
any old way will do. That was what was, in
essence, wrong with the world.

So, now. The things that were happening to her
sounded right, every one of them, although each was
slightly unexpected. Ever so slight. But she had the

odd feeling that she had become the center of some kind of attention. Certainly not from anyone at work. They had no reason to be subtle, and in fact weren't. Perhaps some sort of secret investigation? That was possible, because of Igor, or Afanasy, but if so, they would hardly do it through the foreigner, Maksim, or the situation he represented.

There was something there, she felt, that she was supposed to see—or discover. What was it? It was transparent, on the surface: it was Change, and Mila distrusted change. But something more than that. She thought, trying to reach for it. What was it?

Putting a computer in to do all the tasks that people did, that was the project. That was it. The people. What would happen to all those people? They said that the system was expensive, but it would save the cost of labor. There was something wrong with that, too. It began to become too complicated to hold in her mind. She made a list of things:

1. *Where do the displaced people go?*

2. *Other people will have to take care of the new machines, and it was her experience that the fancier the machine was, the more expensive people it needed to keep it running.*

3. *Where would the spare parts come from? From the United Provinces? What if there was a war somewhere?*

And then Maksim himself. No harm there, not willfully. He was just a technician, nothing more. He was a person who installed systems. He did not work on the consequences—that wasn't his job. She remembered from her childhood when the man from the Ministry of Agriculture had come around, urging everyone to grow the new Barley, a better producer, so they said. And so it had been. Everyone had planted it, and the bins were filled, there had never been such a harvest. And that Winter and the next year, there had been incredible misery, because the price of Barley had fallen and fallen. There was too much, they said. People became poor and lost their land to the taxman and the moneylender. Poverty in the midst of plenty. They had had a revolution, then, too, which had thrown out the old Steel Guard, and brought in the Narodny Sobor. Hard times, indeed.

But what part was she supposed to play in all this? That was what made her uneasy. Mila had learned, partly from Igor, and from her own self-reliance, to look for the pattern underlying things, learn to sidestep trouble. That was the way of it. These events made what she called a pattern in her mind, but it made no sense, and she couldn't see who was arranging it. It seemed inescapable: somebody or something was tampering, tinkering. She was tempted to imagine that it was God doing this, but Mila was not especially religious, and it didn't seem like the sort of thing God was supposed to be interested in. She thought her past with Igor or her present with Afanasy would have made for a much more interesting situation, but who, after all, could argue preferences?

She stopped short at that. *I don't like this line of thinking at all. It wants to lead me into either insanity or religion, and while both those are easy answers,*

*they're both wrong, and . . . designed that way,
sleight of hand, a magician's trick! No, I don't like
it, God's not a trickster, whatever else He may be,
and I won't admit to being crazy when this has
worked for me, every time before, when I had nobody
to tell me anything.* She considered discussing this
with Protopresbyter Zosim, the parish priest, who
was noted as somewhat of a theologian. Yes. And
also, she thought, with Afanasy, too. He was certainly as godless as the rest of the university students,
but he could tie a fine knot in one's head. If she
could keep him talking, and keep his hands off her
long enough to tell her something. He had been
talking about something like this one night. But however it went, she'd have to weigh them carefully,
because one still had only oneself to depend on.

Constantin slid his chair back from the typewriter,
making a raucous scraping noise at which he winced.
He was shaking. He had wanted to set up a relatively simple situation about conflicting loyalties, and
of course, Consequences of Technology, all of which
would have made up a nice, easy story, something
with room to speculate. And then, out of the fabric
of the story, out of the native texture of a fictional
character, uneducated and unsophisticated, comes
this incredible suspicious Mila, and now he was
fallen off the deep end into speculative theology, a
nightmare field filled with devils as well as kindly
spirits. Now too late he saw the trap he had built,
line by line: *to give Mila Vekshin the power to
perceive through the veils of illusion in her world,*

*he also had to give her the power to become aware
of him.* A chill passed along his spine. Constantin
thought that Mila couldn't see him yet, in actuality,
but she knew he was there. He felt guilty. There
was no way out for him, and none for Mila, either.
He hadn't intended that, either.

But then he sat back, laughing at himself. *What
the hell could she do about it, even if she did "see"
me?* Constantin decided to turn in for the night, and
pushed the typewriter back with a sense of finality.

During the next day at work, Mila watched Maksim
carefully, evaluating his remarks and petty betrayals
for conformity with the model she had built in her
mind. For the most part, he remained guileless and
direct, and fit the image well. He also revealed more
than he might have thought he had, and so by noon
Mila had been able to discover who had been the
official who had sponsored Maksim and his project.
She winced when she found it out: it had been
Dekorcak, an untitled but ominously powerful functionary of the Ministry of the Interior. Even so, he
wasn't inaccessible, and by a few careful contacts,
she was able to make an appointment. She promised
her contact that a short letter would precede her visit;
this she wrote out, explaining her misgivings about
the project and the numbers of people it would involve,
and dispatched it by the regular interministry courier.
So far, so good. By the end of the day, she felt
apprehensive, but she also felt a strong sense of
accomplishment. It certainly was not for her to solve
these difficult problems of values and priorities, and

so whatever happened, she had done rightly to bring these questions to the attention of a powerful official like Simon Dekorcak.

She stalled Maksim's invitation once more and left work alone. But this time, she did not stand by the tram stop in Vladny Prospekt, but set off through the streets of Jelusidac westwards into the university quarter.

Mila walked purposefully, passing through deep streets of shops and offices as the light fell, moving with a certain sense of fatalistic abandon. Yes. Other times she had also come this way after work, too, with other errands and other desires in mind; she knew the way well enough.

Afanasy took part-time employment as a bartender in a tavern on a side street, which was called The Dusty Drum, its name now an out-of-fashion reminder of the days when the students had often revolted against the excesses of the Steel Guard. Now, of course, those reactions were long out of favor, but they were beginning to re-emerge and be respectable among the new students.

At this time of day, The Dusty Drum was quiet. It had actually been a cellar at one time, and still had the massive stone pillars supporting the floors above. She stepped inside and down, feeling foolish and vastly out of place in her civil-service uniform. But when she looked over the scattering of students who were already gathered in that place for the night, they seemed in their way no less preposterous, with their absurd collection of bizarre hats and castoff army greatcoats, never mind which army. Later, she knew, musicians would come and fill the bandstand in the corner, and girls with garish makeup would come and join the sulking young men. She found Afanasy at the bar, polishing glass mugs.

It was clear that he hadn't expected her, and he had an uncharacteristically vacant expression on his face, but when he saw it was Mila, he brightened immediately. Mila sat aggressively on a stool, like a customer, and held out her hand as if she expected him to fill it with a mug of beer immediately, without question. It was so convincing that Afanasy drew a glass mug full of pale beer and put it in her outstretched hand. The glass mug was cold. In the poor light behind the bar, Afanasy looked sallow and tired. She thought that he was really out of place in a cellar tavern like this, but she also knew with complete conviction that there was nothing she could do about it.

He said, "I am glad you came. We never see enough of each other."

Mila sipped the beer, which was clear and bitter and very cold. And very good, suddenly. "So you are working tonight?"

"Unfortunately, yes."

"Something came along that I have not understood so well." She always felt guilty about being so cold to Afanasy when they met by chance in public; but they had always been realistic about what passed between them. They looked at each other as odd but delicious vices which were generally harmless and could be tolerated so long as there was no scandal.

He looked almost strabismically along his long

nose and said, softly, as if talking to himself, "It's not like you to come to me for advice."

"Once, you were talking about your friends, and you were talking about a crazy writer. What was his name?"

"All my friends could be called 'crazy writers' of one stripe or another, and I am not sure I should call them friends, either. Which one? I have told you a thousand tales of noble arts trampled, et cetera, pearls before swine, and the like."

Mila sighed in exasperation. *Drunk again!* " This one had written, or was going to write, a tale about a . . . creature who wrote another tale."

Afanasy held up a finger. "Aha! Just so! That one I remember: it was Timofey Smerecky. Now there's an odd one, even in here. His tale was called *God is a Humorist.*"

"Yes, that one."

"Well, he never got it published—which is exactly what you said would come of it. As usual, you were right. Mila, you are a heroine. Do you realize what a weight it is to be right when being wrong is so easy, like falling off a stump? Indeed, I marvel! Yes, you were right. Right." He paused in his recitation, which he was enjoying immensely, because it drove Mila insane when he would not come to the point. "Still, what are we all but the sum total of our obsessions?" He leaned across the bar counter and leered at her.

Mila ignored it all. She expected as much, indeed, worse, and was glad he was as lucid as he was. She had seen him worse. Yes. In this place, she could expect such nonsense. She asked, "I wonder if you could arrange for me to have a talk with him?"

Afanasy suddenly became more awake, but whether from ordinary jealousy or some other suspicion she could not tell. "When? Tonight?"

"Tonight. That would be fine."

He sniffed, morosely. "To tell the truth, I haven't seen him in weeks. They say he's been working somewhere . . . one says in Estoty, another, somewhere off in the East. Well, even great ironists have to locate bread for their board, even if their board is nothing more than the top of an apple crate."

"I remembered you talking about him, but the story . . . I dismissed it at the time, but now I want you to help me remember it. I have part of it, but it won't come out right."

Afanasy leaned back. "Stay until midnight. Then we'll go off somehwere and talk all night, if need be."

"I'd like to. But I can't. I have to be awake tomorrow. To go to a meeting with Dekorcak. I shouldn't want to stroll in there looking like something the dog brought home."

"Dekorcak! What are you doing with him?"

"It's simple. Something came up at work. I saw a situation, and I asked to see him about it, when I found out he was the one who had set the whole thing in motion."

"You asked? Around here, they claim to have plague to avoid talking to him."

"I know he has some standing, but . . ."

"Standing! Standing, indeed! He's the chief of the Secret Police, the *Obarona*."

"I heard those tales . . . I always thought them just political slogans."

"No slogans to it. Dangerous. Those kind, you don't even ask questions of."

"Well, it can't be helped now."

Afanasy shook his head. "All right. But be careful, whatever it is, will you."

"I thought that if I were right, if I had seen something they needed to know, they would reward me." She was oddly defensive, now, subdued.

Afansy shook his head from side to side. "Right, wrong . . . Mila, how many times have I told you those things don't matter anymore. They don't see *right* and *wrong*. They see *For* and *Against*. You'll go in there with whatever you thought up, and I know you well enough to know it's sincere, and he'll think 'just another damned attitude case.' That's at best."

"Well, I've already done it, so I have to go through with it." But for once, as happened rarely, Mila saw and felt a strong sense of truth in Afanasy, just as she saw the concern and fear written plainly on his face. And she also saw that his perception of Dekorcak was more correct than hers. She had, indeed, been foolish. But she waited, looking off into the dark corners of the tavern and then said, "Never mind. The novel, then. That has nothing to do with Dekorcak, but it's part of something else. Tell me again."

"All right. It went like this: Timka was lecturing one day, about making a character live by giving it free will, and it occurred to him out of the blue that maybe God created the world by the process of writing a large and ponderous novel, yes, perhaps a very bad novel: Hugo, Zola, de Maupassant, who knows? And then the situation that would arise from that—who was real, and what sorts of barriers separated them? How could the writer communicate with the characters?''

''That's . . . crazy!''

''No, wait, hear me out; it's not so crazy as it seems. Listen: this was Timofey's argument. Who's real? What's the different between a fictional story and the history of a hundred years ago? Of a hundred years yet to be?''

Mila looked across the bar as if confronting a madman. She said, ''Real people leave behind real effects; characters in a story are only that.''

''Wrong. Some real people, so to speak, vanish without a trace, while some characters not only create real effects, but sometimes influence large numbers of people. So who's more real? So went the argument. And more; Timofey argued that this 'tale' might not be published, or else if it was, then it would get bad reviews. Indeed, if it were realistic, you could guarantee that it would get bad reviews. The implications are horrific.''

Mila looked up at the sooty ceiling and then back to Afanasy. There was no doubt about it. The whole crowd of them were mad as hatters. She said, ''Well, if it really were like Timofey says, then there would be no problem, because this writer could write in anything he wanted.''

"Oh, no, there's the rub! He *could* . . . but he doesn't dare. Because you have to give everything depth and a sort of independence, otherwise the story has neither life nor meaning—it's just wooden, perhaps plastic. All these things extend outside the story into areas you never see, but they exist nonetheless. And all of them have to act to some degree *on their own*: sometimes good, sometimes evil, sometimes irrationally. They gain momentum that way, mass, weight, depth. He could make a lion eat grass, but once he writes in a lion, it has power to remain itself. *The world he creates has power over him*. And because the story is a condensation, an emphasizing, of the writer's world, it's more vivid, and in the end more powerful than his own proper world. The more perfect the work, the less minute-to-minute control the creator has. And in the end, he has to try to reach his own characters, and he does so by a certain pattern of mistakes, overcontrol, oddities. I don't wonder that Timofey can't get the thing published; only he could come up with something like that."

Mila sat silently for a long time. Then she said, quietly, "It's true."

"What's true?"

She hastily added, "That only Timofey could say that."

"Is that what you wanted to hear?"

"Yes. Thank you—you have done me a real favor."

"I have more to say, and not about novels, either."

Mila blushed, and felt the hot flash flowing up into her face. "I know. And I might like to hear some of them, too. But not tonight. Please understand."

Afanasy nodded, solemnly. "Just so. But why did you want to hear that story?"

"Something I saw reminded me of it, but I couldn't remember how it went. You didn't say all that much the first time."

"You are as opaque as one of those frosted-glass office doors they favor in the ministries, and mysterious as well. But never mind, never mind! I will tell Timofey you asked, if and when I see him again. It would please him—he has few enough fans."

"No, no! I didn't say I agreed! I just wanted to hear how it went, that's all. And a fine job you did!" She tipped up the mug and finished off the remanants of the beer.

"Do you remember how to get home from here?"

"Yes. I can manage. Do the trams still run out here at night?"

"Yes."

"Then I will go home, now. And . . . please give me some time alone for a while. Not forever, but a little bit. There are some things I need to have all my attention on."

She said the last so sincerely, so earnestly, that Afanasy leaned over the bar. "Are you in trouble?"

"Not yet."

"Do you need a place to go? Such things can be arranged."

"No. Don't worry. I survived before, and I'll make do now. Believe me. I know what I have to do."

She touched his hand, briefly, slid off the stool, and turned to leave the cellar. As Mila was making her way to the door, a girl came in, of a delicate, fragile build, with chalk-white mime's makeup, black lipstick and fingernails. She halted and stared in astonishment at the departing figure of Mila, in her maroon uniform, walking as if with a great weight on her, now absorbed in her own thoughts. The girl hurried to the bar, where she addressed Afanasy. "Did you see that! Were we inspected?"

Afanasy smiled vacantly and said, "It was nothing. A beer-inspectress."

The girl looked back to the door with an exaggerated motion, wonderingly, where Mila had already vanished into the damp night outside. She turned back. "Did we pass?"

"Grade number one. Primo!"

Mila was possessed of no such assurances. The tram which ran from the university quarter to her part of the city, Soblaznaya, wound all around and passed through all sorts of places, some of them not so savory. It generally followed the winding course of the River Syrma, and tonight it seemed that an unhealthy damp mist rose from the narrow little cut, the Mokrodola, in which the river ran. It was not fog. Mila would have thought of that as mysterious and romantic. This was just a damp that gathered in a shabby fashion about the streetlights and concealed suspicious odors and wafts of organic substances.

She stepped off at the corner where the neighborhood church stood. By the light of the streetlamp, bleak and harsh, St. Melchiades looked desolated, abandoned, left for the wreckers. The houses and buildings which had surrounded it had long since been torn down, and so it remained on the corner, alone and exposed, an odd L-shaped edifice with a broad silvered dome at the intersection of its two wings, a large and imposing steep flight of granite steps leading up to the narrow portico. The lamps inside were out. One block away, a complex of weaving factories sprawled down the hill, their sawtooth-roof vent windows brightly lit from within. She paused for a moment, half-hoping she might run into Protopresbyter Zosim on his way to or from a late vigil, but the only living being she could see were three loud drunks down by the factories, singing and making extravagant claims. She hurried on.

Once safely home, she skipped supper, munching on a leftover bagel, and even hurried through her bath, reaching for the security of darkness, the lights out, the door bolted, the dim light from the corner streetlight seeping in around the curtains. It was late. But even with the coverlet pulled over her head, sleep wouldn't come, and she moved her body, now suddenly heavy and unmanageable, from one position to another. Her mind raced, filled with images of Dekorcak, Maksim. Masinen, and of an unknown, unimaginable Somebody, somewhere and somewhen, who wrote out worlds in which existed such as Jelusidac, triangular railroad terminals, Ministries of the Interior, Igor Vekshin, Afanasy, herself. How would one address such an entity? And if one could, what would one ask? For success? Wealth? She shuddered, terrified. *No, none of that.* She would say, loudly and clearly, *Leave me alone! Leave us alone!* She suddenly wanted Afanasy very much, like strong drink, intensely, wantonly. She thought, irrelevantly, *The next time he comes, I'll fix him a nice dinner.*

Constantin looked out the window to the bare trees which obscured his view down the hill to the little commercial district. He looked with a bleary eye, backed by a tremendous headache. He had been up all night. He turned wearily from the window and shuffled like a drunkard into the bathroom, where he removed a small packet from the medicine cabinet, stretched it into a stiff tube, and emptied the bitter contents into his mouth. He washed the potion down with a glass of water, and went to bed, his head still ringing. He felt embarrassed, ashamed of himself, a dirty old man caught peeking through a hole in the wall of the girls' gymnasium, moreover, a hole he had laboriously made himself over a long time. *This was not going well at all.* He really did not want to argue epistemology with Mila, ontology, ophthalmology or anthropology. And most especially he did not want her to perceive why he felt this way. After all, he did have control of the story. Didn't he?

Mila arrived slightly early for her appointment with Dekorcak. He kept his offices in a nondescript old building on one of the older, narrow streets leading off the Prospekt, a dark stone edifice of no distinction whatsoever. But it did, inside, have fine high ceilings, and, judging by the few doors she passed, large, spacious rooms. It was also quiet. Not silent: there were people about, going about their errands in a perfectly normal manner. And to her surprise, she did not have to wait, but was sent in immediately.

Dekorcak sat at a plain, openfront desk, with the windows behind him, toward the center of a large room. The room was quite bare, not at all as she might have imagined it. To her left, on one wall was a tea-cupboard with a brass samovar. The rug was an old floral print, now quite threadbare. To her right, on the other wall, hung portraits, somewhat retouched, photographs of the members of the Praesidium of the Narodny Sobor: Volzhankin, Sobakevic, Tsygana, Radikal'ny and Brodyagin. To a man, they all managed to convey the impression of being reprimanded schoolmasters, righteous and chastened and fussy all at once. Dekorcak did not resemble them: he was an almost-elderly, plump, bald man with a fringe of white hair who wore steel-rimmed spectacles. A country doctor. She had to remind herself forcibly who he really was.

When she came in, he had been reading from a folder on the desk. He continued reading, looked up, and said, mildly, "Please be seated. Relax." He continued reading for a moment, and then looked at her again. Now he said, "You are Ludmila Vekshin, a senior clerk in the Ministry of Railroad Communications."

"Yes."

"You have expressed some concern over the consequences of installing the new monitoring and control system."

"Yes."

"We have found your conclusions to be both perceptive and well-presented. Altogether excellent. No one anticipated such ability. Nothing in your background. Where did you uncover such an idea?"

"I saw that there were things in the program which had not been considered or planned for. So it seemed. At first I dismissed it, but the more I thought, the more I thought I should bring it to someone's attention."

"Why not your nominal supervisor, Masinen?"

"Administrator Masinen had stressed to me more than once that he did not make decisions, but rather implemented them. Through the conversations I had with the Technician Maksim, I understood that you were the sponsor of his project."

Dekorcak nodded, absentmindedly, and made some notes on a pad. "Just so. I believe you came to the Capital from Dubnovo Province. You had married a Captain of Armor, one Igor Vekshin."

"Yes, that is correct."

"Vekshin subsequently became involved in a scandal of sorts, some embarassing events, was reduced to the ranks, and posted to the East."

"Yes."

"You were not aware of the nature of his difficulties?"

"I heard some things, and I was told other things. None of it made much sense, frankly. It was a difficult time for me, and I did not bother untangling things. I had decisions to make on my own, and of course I was totally on my own."

"You are still legally married to Vekshin."

"That is true; however, I have applied for official Separation, and a decree of Divorcement for reasons of abandonment and non-support."

Again that subtle nod. "Quite so. Do you have any communications with Vekshin?"

"No. For a time, he sent me some money, but that stopped."

"Did you make inquiries?"

"Yes. There was no answer. As I said, things were difficult, and I had little time to wait. I felt as if he might have gotten into more trouble."

"Yes, of course. And now you have a lover, a certain Afanasy Nedotykomkin. I believe a part-time student at the University."

Mila felt her face redden, and a deep chill far down in her lower back, almost in her buttocks. *So this was what real fear felt like!* She felt naked; they knew *everything*. But with the fear also came a strong feeling of empathy with Igor, as if this situation was one he had known well. It was almost as if he were with her, somewhere in her mind. A presence. As if he were there in the room, facing Dekorcak with her. She was ashamed to have this fragile phantom presence hear these revelations, but the sense of presence did not seem to mind at all. It was as if he said to her, *Keep quiet and don't volunteer information! Make him work for it. Afanasy is vermin, but even he is preferable to Dekorcak.*

Dekorcak now asked, "Do you view this relationship as permanent, long-lasting?"

"No. I was lonely. Things . . . just happened."

The ghostly presence in her mind seemed to say, not in words but in feelings, *Even taking a lover is preferable to kissing an official's arse.* She felt some of his strangled rage even now, something she had almost forgotten. She hadn't understood it, then.

"But you do not keep company with him or his friends."

"No."

"I don't imagine you would . . . But you did make inquiries about a Timofey Smerecky."

"Yes, I did."

"Why?"

"It was something I wanted to remember. Not really connected with the new project. I thought of it, and I wanted to remember it. The first time Afanasy told me I wasn't listening very well."

Her answer seemed to disorient him slightly, as if it fit none of the categories he had previously established. He said, after a moment, "Most curious. You are aware that they think very highly of you over in the Tower."

"I understood that it was an honor to be assigned to work with Maksim."

"And so it was. Deserved, too. And because the objections you have raised were and are most pertinent, I will try to answer them as best as I can. It is simple. This decision was made at the very highest levels. We must become modernized—this is the way things are done in the most advanced states. They displace workers without a thought, so then it must work. It will have to be that way here. We will adjust. Essentially, that is the way of it."

Dekorcak stopped, as if to collect his thoughts. But what he had said sounded not only wrong, but toally irrational, almost a selection of random utterances, rather than a speech. Mila could not believe that an official could be so powerful, had attained such a position, and yet could be so stupid or disorganized. Or, more sinisterly, was it *because* they were stupid and uncaring that they rose, not in spite of. The only explanation was unspeakable, and she could hardly think it. Her mind reeled. They *wanted* the workers displaced and uprooted. Why? That would only bring in the very miseries they had sworn to heal. Unless they wanted, in the future, a number of loose people, for which they would have a use, and then they'd do whatever it was, willingly. . . . She didn't know how she had seen that, but however it had been she very much did not want Dekorcak to know that she had even imagined it for a moment. She was much more frightened now than she had been at Dekorcak's knowledge of her personal life.

He said, as if musing aloud, "These modern systems are intricate and difficult to understand. At present, we are dependent on the skills of foreigners. It might be useful to have one of our own people knowledgeable about these things."

He stopped, as if waiting for some comment, or an answer, but Mila looked at him as blankly as she could manage, as if she had no idea where he was going.

He said, in a soft voice, "On the recommendation from the proper level, I believe that you would qualify for such a position."

She had wondered what form it would take. An offer or a threat. This was an offer, but it had the same effect. *Either way it's all the same,* the presence in her mind reminded her. *Take it, fool, you won't get a second offer. They buy them off or beat them with a whip, it's all the same.* Mila thought a moment, and then said, "I would have to go to school. We have no such schools."

"That is correct."

"I could not travel to a foreign country; I am still married legally to Igor Vekshin, a National of our State."

"But you had applied for an Act of Divorcement."

"Yes, of course."

"It was approved this morning. Do you wish to retain the surname 'Vekshin'?"

For a moment, her heart stopped. "Yes."

"The necessary ecclesiastical permissions are now being approved as well, a mere formality, I assure you. The Holy Synod has already concurred in principle. This was a most unfortunate case, which I am happy to have been instrumental in resolving in the interest of the communal best interest." He leafed through the folders on his desk, and produced a small sheaf of papers, which he handed across the desk to Mila. "Here, I believe, are the pertinent documents. Take care of them, if you please."

Mila took them, speechless, but she did not dare look at them. Not then. She would look at them later. Dekorcak said, "In the meantime, please continue your excellent work with Maksim. This is a project of great importance and must go forward as planned. I am sure that you understand."

"Yes." And the memories of Igor spoke for him, saying, *Now, good! Walk out and don't look back. Don't ask any questions, none at all. No matter what.* She wanted to ask what had happened to Igor. He knew. But she did not dare. And she was not sure she wanted to know. There was a price to knowing. She said, "Thank you. You understand that this is very sudden, unexpected."

"Of course, of course. But we felt you would find the idea attractive. You have done well, and in a just world, excellence should and must be rewarded, don't you think?"

"Please express my gratitude to those responsible."

"Be assured that I will. And now, if you will excuse me, there are other pressing matters I must attend to. You are familiar with the saying that to get a thing done, one must give it to a busy man."

Mila nodded, absentmindedly, and got up, clutching her documents, to leave the office. She walked out of the old building automatically, finding her way without thinking, without a word, without a single glance aside. She had passed some threshold, she knew, and had become a creature of passage, a sailor on a sea as strange as the seas which had confronted Ulysses. She bitterly recalled the memory of Igor which had now faded almost beyond existence, *You would be ashamed at the toady I have become. All that, and a tart as well, the mistress of a never-do-well student revolutionary.* She was ashamed of herself; Dekorcak had played her so easily.

But after a moment, crossing the Prospekt to return to work, the presence seemed to return, although much weaker than before. It was as if it said, *Not so at all! As we might have said in the Regiment, Molodets! Good fellow! You have done well! Now keep your mouth shut and take it and run—it's your only chance. You have six weeks. And take Afanasy with you. It's all in those papers.*

She thought back angrily, *Afanasy is worthless!*

It answered, *You now have the power to make him worthy.*

What about you?

I'll settle my own affairs. I am beyond your power to help me.

She was still walking across the broad expanses of Vladny Prospekt, but now nearing the Terminal. She ventured a question to the ghostly presence once more: *Maybe I could just go and stay in the United Provinces. Surely they don't live like this, there.*

Igor answered, *It's all the same wherever you go.*

Constantin knew well enough when was the proper moment to let it go. That was one of the secrets: knowing when to stop. Any fool could start speaking, and keep on. Now the story had "resolved" and there was nothing more to be done about it. Of course he could rewrite it, but then it would be another story, with an equally unforeseen resolution. No. For better or worse, Mila and her world had done all they could, at least for now. *Art was a window into another world.* Constantin called events like these "crucial life events," and in actual fact there never were very many of them in any person's life, real or realistic-fictional. He could, of course, continue to track Mila's life, but it might be years in her time before something else might turn up worth writing about. And that, too, was true of a realistic character who had, so to speak, "come to life." Whatever one said, people weren't space cadets, they never had one adventure after another. They stepped up to their chalk marks on the stage, said their lines, and stepped off, professionally, and then went back to finding a place to live, buying groceries. Secretly, though, he felt a certain sense of chagrin, a shadowy feeling of male inadequacy, because at the crucial moment, Mila had listened to Igor, instead of him, the creator of her world.

He had invited Anna and Ramon over to celebrate, and had a nice, finished, proofed manuscript for them to read while the rolls were browning in the oven. It was Dimančo, in the early afternoon, and the sky, previously cloudy, had cleared nicely. Bright sunlight was streaming in through the tall windows.

After lunch, Constantin listened while both Anna and Ramon expressed their feelings about the story. They were mostly congratulatory. He heard them out, and then said, "I can see that it works well enough, that Mila is very lifelike, rather more than most characters, but I was unable from the beginning to have the control I wanted. As it was, I sometimes felt as if what little I was doing was intruding too much. She almost could see me. Besides, I wanted to make it more pointed, the issue of the demeaning effects of technology."

Ramon exclaimed, with some heat, "Not so! You did very well! Technology itself—well, that's just a tool, isn't it? It's the people who are noble like eagles or vile like batrachians."

Anna said, "Mila is a very strong character; she creates a whole world around her, as if by some force field."

Constantin huffed. "Creates a world? A tacky, Balkan world, more suited to a popular operetta. I half-expected, at any moment, that some fruitcake character would come leaping out of the wings in an admiral's uniform, spouting some nonsense about being 'The Tiger of the Adriatic, Scourge of Durazzo, Master of the Straits of Otranto'!"

Ramon, who was given to excess, said, "Mila was such a person, and well-done, too! She exposed for the reader the lives of degenerate bureaucrats. If you had to deal with them in real life, indeed you would believe in retrograde evolution!"

Anna added, "It must go as it is. I insist."

Constantin looked off, through the windows. "It didn't do what I wanted it to do."

Anna retorted, "That doesn't matter! It does something. You say you write speculative surrealism: very well. You have speculated legitimately and well."

Constantin retorted, "Yes, but about theology, for God's sake. About government."

Anna said, "So what! Mila has something to tell us."

Ramon asked, leering, "Did she take Afanasy?"
His sympathies always were with the rum characters.

Art is a window into another world. And so stories
are not themselves whole worlds, but only pieces of
those worlds, only a part that shows, if they are
done well. But it is to be understood that they have
antecedent parts that run back to Creation itself,
the Prime Singularity—and continuations that run
on to the end of time. Somewhere, Mila Vekshin
lives on. No, Mila was not a space cadet.

Mila stood by the rail of the steamer as it puttered
its slow way across the shallow Estotian Sea toward the Aland Islands, from which they would
travel onward to the United Provinces. Afanasy stood
beside her. She had turned in her maroon uniforms,
but she had kept the sensible shoes. One never
knew. Still, she wore a raincoat and hid her luxuriant brown hair under a dark kerchief.

It was Spring, now, but there, on the sea, there
was yet a damp chill in the air. People passed by
along the deck behind them, walking back and forth
to stay warm and to keep from becoming seasick.
They were speaking in all sorts of impossible
languages. She listened for a time, fascinated. Then
she heard familiar speech. She did not dare turn to
see who it was.

"So who else did you see while you were in
prison?"

(Gruff voice) "We had the writer Smerecky in our
group for a while, but then they shipped him back

to some work-program back in real life. He found prison funny and they couldn't stand it. Then there was Vekshin.''

"You were in with Vekshin? How did that go? We heard that he was dead!''

(Gruff voice) "Indeed! But he was alive, then. You know, he had always been defiant. Roared like a lion. They broke him, of course. They always go for the resisters, and the more you resist, the harder they try. You become a goal, a challenge, and they, the scum, have endless time. So they did. He came out of remand block, but he died two weeks later.''

"Of what? beatings?''

(Gruff voice) "No, no, I don't think so. It was as if he were trying to last just long enough, and then he just gave up. Stared at the light bulb. But he was smiling.''

"When was that?'' (Voice fading now)

"About two years. . . .''

Alarmed, Mila looked around sharply, trying now to match the voices with the dull backs she saw retreating up the deck. Dark dull pants, heavy nondescript coats, flat workmen's caps. There was no knowing— they all looked the same. She looked at Afanasy, who had also heard, and had a sober look to him. Her eyes sparkled, misted over.

He looked after the departing figures and said, "I heard. I can do no less.''

Mila looked out over the railing to the sea, and to the indistinct horizon, where the pale green sea met the pale green sky without visible demarcation.

ENTERTAINMENT

Of all the stories in this book, this is the only
one which has a previous printing history: it was first
published in New Voices 4, edited by George R. R.
Martin.

That was in 1981. Actually, the story itself
has been around since the early seventies in various
lengths and guises. True to form, I cannot resist
tinkering with it, so discerning readers will doubtless
find some small changes here and there.

**For Suzanne, who played Faero, or perhaps
vice-versa.**

The whole secret is to know how to set about it, to
be able to concentrate the mind on a single point, to
obtain a suffcent degree of self-abstraction to
produce the necessary hallucination and so substi-
tute the vision of reality for the reality itself.

—J. K. Huysmans, *A Rebours,* 1884

Cormen Demir-Hisar settled himself carefully in his contour chair, at first facing the door; he tipped it with his foot into a slow rotation to his left, to face the view-window, picking up the window control handset as he moved. He dialed in the code setting for city-now, center reference this house in an unobstrusive corner of the Crithote Hills, no magnification, normal spectrum, azimuth 090°. The south wall of the room, a slick gray surface, momentarily shimmered, trembled, and suddenly became transparent, just as if there had been no wall there, but a perfect window.

It was afternoon and the shadows were falling in long slants across the east, the direction he had chosen. He could see across the panorama of the city—a view of low, plain towers, pastel domes, the foliage of carefully tended trees: umbrella pine, poinciana, laburnum, giant lagerstroemia, Madagascar palms, columnar cypress. Beyond the city could be glimpsed the shimmer of the river through the foliage, and farther still, beyond the river, the browngold hills and swales of the Dawnlands rolled away to the limits of vision. The sun illuminated everything with a clear, golden, late-afternoon light, and the sky was cloudless and cobalt-blue.

City-now. The real world, just as it came, a view to the east. He could have selected many other scenes, some merely casually, as a curious excursion; others he called for again and again, so often that he had arranged to have special precoding set up for them so as to avoid the tiresome necessity of dialing in the entire reference code: *Mount Everest by*

Moonlight, Point Lobos Surf, Moorea Dawn, The Sea of Grass, Persepolis at Sundown, The Barque Kurt *Going Around Cape Horn in a Squall.* These, and thousands more. But when he did his most serious work, he always perferred to have city-now, east, in the window. It seemed to help focus his attention.

For some time, Cormen had enjoyed a peculiar suspicion, which he had learned from his wanderings around the city, and cultivated with a little notebook, in which he had made a detailed series of notes and jottings, as well as crude, but effective, charts and maps of certain districts. "Cormen's Problem," as it was known, was familiar to the members of the circle in which he moved; in fact, if he had not been so effective with his productions and so engaging in his personality, they might have considered him a bore.

It seemed, so the suspicion went, that the city was slowly shrinking, as evidenced by abandoned districts along the city edges. Beyond the empty houses were ruins, and beyond that, traces of foundations and street lines. Moreover, it had recently dawned on him that there were no roads out of the city, although there were no restraints. One hardly noticed this—it was the norm. But like many an easy assumption, once broken it became increasingly obvious.

Cormen's acquaintances were tolerant of his aberration, but generally unsympathetic. What he needed was proof, something he could demonstrate in black and white—and color if required. But the city was reluctant, so it appeared, to give up its realities so easily. The Master Entertainment Center, MEC, would not answer direct queries about this, even though it would obediently show him presentations, pictorial or symbolic as he required, of the areas in question. But it was tiresome detail work, in which he had to proceed completely on his own.

Here is how it could begin: Cormen began arranging his notes in an order, from which supplementary instructions could be sent to MEC for additional information. Specificity, that was the word. But before he could properly begin, a soft belling chime from the communicator interrupted the flow of his thoughts.

The chime broke the silence of the house: a caller, requesting a contact. Who could it be now? Cormen put his notes on the floor beside him, and rotated the chair another ninety degrees left to face the reception plate. He said, aloud, "Answer!"

The receptor, apparently an oval mirror, hung with its long axis parallel to the floor, and was mounted in an elaborate baroque gilded frame, ornamented with cherubs, garlands of flowers, and cornucopias discharging streams of fruit. At the upper center of the frame, a red telltale glowed; when Cormen spoke, it turned first yellow, then green. The mirror surface flowed like smoke, then cleared, to transmit an image of a pleasant garden adjacent to the rustic house, inhabited by a young woman of remarkable beauty who sat at an umbrella-shaded table with a tall frosted glass close at hand. She was of no identifiable age, but was tall, graceful, and possessed of a ripe, curved figure. Her complexion was a dark, suntanned olive, with black hair cascading in waves and ripples down her shoulders. The face was aquiline, the eyes a deep brown the color of liver. Cormen knew her well: Nilufer Emeksiz.

Cormen said, to the mirror, "So you have moved a portable unit out into the garden for today's calls!"

The woman nodded and smiled, and touched a control beside her, causing the image to zoom in closer. "Yes! I always make my best calls from the garden! And there you are at home, shut in like a hermit, when all sorts of *sobrany** are either in progress, or are anxiously anticipated."

Cormen always felt dull and superfluous before the ebullient Nilufer, an inveterate party-goer and attender of *sobrany*. He smiled back, and said, "I haven't been shut up all day—I took a stroll this morning. And I plan this very evening to wander over by Embara Park, to see what might turn up. You know how I am—I prefer to be . . . well, not quite so intense."

"It's true! You are a hermit! A veritable anchorite! A wall-eyed, bat-eared misanthrope! But people are always asking for you, do you know? They say, 'Please ask Cormen to come, please do, he always add such substance to a *sobrana*.' I don't know how you do it, really. I have to do exercises, stay in fighting trim all the time—and yet you perch up there

---

Sobrany, sing. *sobrana*. Lit., a meeting. This was a semi-public social function very much like a restrained party, during which things of value were exchanged, and rendezvous arranged.

in Crithote Hills, now and again to sally forth with another astonishing display of viewpoint-indeces*, or else some marvelous production which everyone wants to subscribe to." She turned down the corners of her soft mouth. "Well—I suppose searching them out as well as you do, does take some time."

Cormen smiled back at the image of Nilufer and said, "Everyone must search out their own best work. Besides, my real vice is curiosity, as I am often reminded. It is true."

Nilufer asked, suddenly serious, "Are you still pursuing that thing you were worried about, about . . . what was it? The city is shrinking, yes? Why, that's like saying, 'The sky is falling.' "

---

*Viewpoint indices—productions. A viewpoint-index is a set of time-space-angle view settings, referring to a specific event, nominally in the past, although this is not an absolute requirement. A view might be a natural formation, a sunset, a city scene, or perhaps wars or natural disasters. Anything at all which could be found with space-time coordinates. *Productions* are, essentially, works of art arranged by the citizens with the aid of MEC, often combining many media, and often transforming the originals into bizarre and unrecognizable forms. Video and music were the most popular forms, but all arts were utilized. An Original Work by a historic artist might be utilized, then developed, but *meta-originals*, works that could have been done, but weren't, were more popular. For example, Beethoven's Tenth Symphony. For example, a novel written after a writer's untimely death. MEC arranged all projections and transformations. All Viewpoint-indeces and productions contained in their encoding-set an address group which routed royalties to the person who had designed the production. Trade in these items constituted the major income of the citizens.

"Yes, that was what I was working on, just now. I am sure of it, but I need confirmation, of course, and that is a most difficult thing to get out of MEC. You know—you can work it in view-mode in one of two ways: City-Now, or Open. In City-Now, there's no time reference, so you can't trace things. Also, the movement program is very slow, so it's hard to move about. You don't have the space coordinates to move around much. Fly it manually, as it were. And when you go to Open mode, you can move about easily, but you can't find the city."

"Cormen, there's a lot of time and space to look about in, in Open mode."

"But no one, to my knowledge, has ever found it."

"Give them time, dear. They are not looking for it. And besides, you do so have time, in City-Now."

"Yes, yes, but it's not scaled time, but reference time: 'Days-ago.' I've tried it: you have to add them up one day at a time, and as far as I have managed to go, it's all the same."

"You haven't gone far enough."

"And if I should, it will take so much time that I know you would call me a hermit, and I wouldn't have time for anything else."

"Who could live that way, Cormen? But for now, you must give up your search."

"How so?"

She continued, breathlessly, "You must drop your plans to cruise Embara Park! Those are low-class atavisms, anyway. And do come to Brasille Sobranamest: Corymont Deghil is hosting a fine soirée, and I have been asked to insure your presence. There! It's done: you must come!''

"Deghil, is it? I'm honored, but how does he know of me?''

"You are by no means as obscure as you might like to think. Just think, Cormen, cruising Embara Park! For shame! But they've heard of you, indeed—some have subscribed. That last one you floated out did it, I think.''

"Which one?''

"Well, I didn't see it, but I heard that it was very strange; something about a king wearing a mask . . .''

"The King in Yellow?"

"Yes, that one.''

Cormen demurred, "I would be surprised at that; you know that the Original doesn't exist, except in fragments of another Original. The Prime Author only referred to it, and included some poems, supposedly scenes from an imaginary play which had the ability to cause dire events. From what we had, I simply had MEC synthesize a real play, and then reprogram it as cinema, in turn run as an animation, based on the style of Virgil Finlay. It was an experiment . . .''

"Well, word has gotten around. And so far, it hasn't caused any dire events, except that Deghil and his associates have been looking up some of your other productions, and he wants to meet you. You have something up your sleeve, I trust?''

"Well, yes, I do have one; it's part of a series I'm

working on. This is the first. I haven't had it out yet, but . . ."

"Oh, no! No cold feet! Do it! Be revolutionary and daring! And do tell me about it, so I can smile knowingly and leer when you tell him. I have implied that I am much in your confidence."

Cormen smiled. "This is a fairly literal version of Robinson Jeffers' poem *Roan Stallion*, performed as a live rock concert by the group Genesis, then filmed. The music turned out particularly good; I specified that they use their full tour regalia, using both new and old guitarists. Got their famous light show, everything. I had it done in an auditorium in Paris, metadate supposedly around 1980. Of course, it had to be simu-assembled, but I think it looks very good."

"You said that it was part of a series?"

"Yes. If this went well, I planned to do all of Jeffers' major long dramatic poems in this way, with Genesis. They seemed particularly well-suited to Jeffers, and no one else had ever tried the combination before."

"I wonder why you didn't do the poem as cinema, I mean, as the story itself, with musical accompaniment? I mean . . ."

"Nilufer, that's what everyone would do. But in some intense kinds of music, the performance of the music itself becomes the drama: this has been so noted in several periods. And so . . ."

"Yes, yes, I know; I work the Rachmaninoff Era myself. But I didn't know that this had also appeared later."

"Oh, yes. Perhaps ever stronger."

"Amazing! You are perverse, but a wonderful perversity it is! And now I must tell you that the day is today, or rather this evening, at the usual time, and . . ."

"And?"

"And, I have another . . . I have a new friend, very recently emerged, who has somehow come across your name and wishes to meet you in person. Oh, you gigolo! She is really very nice, a sweet girl, if a little boyish in the figure, you know. Quiet and polite. One of your 'Second-glancers,' I believe." Here Nilufer was alluding to one of Cormen's habits of preferring girls who he said only showed their attractive qualities on the second glance. Most other people didn't understand the concept; meaning well, they might bring forward girls who were merely plain, or perhaps some who could uncharitably be described as agressively ugly.

"That sounds suspicious . . . But I know you would never sell me to some awful creature."

"But never!"

"But you are always meeting them, aren't you? Well, I like intrigue as well as the next. Does this marvelous creature have a name, or is she to be a woman of total mystery?"

"Faero Sheftali is how she calls herself. And she's a cool one, she is. I offered her your call-code, and she refused it. And, she doesn't give hers out, either. We have been out a couple of times, and she got plenty of offers, but to my knowledge she did not give hers out once. In fact, she said so, to me."

"Well, one doesn't need codes, after all. And the ones in which you get an arbitrary one-time call-code get billed as doubles, you know. If she got so many requests, she could be thinking to do it that way . . . And if that's so, she's not plain, no matter what you say."

Nilufer thought a moment. "That's true. But I still think she's a bit plain. But to do it without handout codes*, you have to use that dreary headset and the damn thing—pardon my emphasis—gives me a splitting headache, and then I don't want to do it when the simula comes, and so the evening's shot! But! I promised Faero I would ask you to come, for her, if not for Deghil; and now you must tell me you will come."

"Tonight, is it? But who am I to come for?"

"Both! Corymont Deghil, for your advancement and your credit balance, and for Faero . . . whatever may transpire!"

---

*Codes . . . simula: Each person had a call-code, by which one could, through MEC, request the company of that person. What actually appeared was called a simula; the simula was indistinguishable from the prime in every way. It was neither known nor questioned how this was done. The purpose of the calls was generally erotic gratification. In the process, the MEC transferred funds from the citizen's credit balance, from caller to callee, and so great store was set upon good appearance and manners. Unable to obtain the desired person's call-code, one could derive a one-time number through MEC, but it cost double, and sometimes caused unpleasant side effects as well, although these could be overcome. This was also a source of income for the citizens.

Cormen laughed. "Very well! I shall come. And since I know so few in that circle, and the new girl—Faero—not at all, I shall look for you. What will you be wearing?"

Nilufer laughed, "Something from the closet! Any old rag!" And the image, clear as if there were no intervening device at all, shimmered, became a smoky, swirling plate, and then a plain mirror again.

Cormen spent the remainder of the afternoon in a nap, knowing that later, in all probability, he would have to be up late, and that he had a work-shift to perform the next day. It was important to appear at these things fresh.

Later, walking along the gracefully curving walkways of the city, Cormen considered his invitation, and what a rare piece of good fortune it had been for him. The circle, of which Corymont Deghil was the nominal head, was generally adjudged the most influential and successful of all, and admission into it could only only be considered as a powerful talisman of long and successful life. He did not feel a sense of apprehension, but an elation, as if his chance, his opening, had finally come. And what of the unknown girl, who had asked for him? Such things were rare, extremely rare, what with all the possibilities there were for selecting a night's partner. Still, it hinted at the unconventional flavor he preferred and tried to find.

Now Cormen reflected again on Deghil: according to rumor, Corymont Deghil was considered extremely knowledgeable about the most productive areas, media, periods and eras in time in which to derive the best programs, in viewpoint-indeces, music, cinema, all the arts. Not only strong in matters of refinement and taste, he was also known to do programs for the more common tastes, popular programs which enjoyed wide acceptance and subscription. And he was reputed to enjoy an enviable credit balance by remaining attractive and dynamic. Indeed, Cormen thought that this was the correct way to proceed; he could feel his own life going that way, in subtle feedbacks, such as the deference Nilufer now used with him, as if he were becoming someone to know. For those reasons, going to this *sobrana* could not fail to be promising. And at any event, he could allay his pet project for a while. It had come to occupy more and more of his attention, even sometimes emitting tantalizing glimpses of a sense of something utterly wrong, completely astray.

Cormen passed a shop where programming information was sold to the totally unknowledgeable; as he passed, he checked his reflection in the glass of the window. He saw in the reflection a young man of slender physique, with a narrow, rather intense face, dressed in suitable attire for the occasion, soft gray pants and tunic, open at the throat, with a maroon night-cape. Everything seemed to be in order.

Along the way, he also passed Embara Park, where the neophytes were already beginning to gather for the evening's exchanges. Here, he himself had begun, and here he frequently returned. Of course, it wasn't what it had been in the old days,

and he missed the flavor of that time, now several
years past. Things had seemed to mean more, then;
people made hard commitments and stuck by them.
Nowadays, they seemed to rely more on what
Cormen thought was cheap sensationalism in their
productions. Some built up a repertoire of morbid
works, other specialized in works depicting violence
or degradation, and still others offered works of
bizarre, ritualistic and deviant sexual practices.
Despite the obvious reproaches, however, he still
came, now and then, to Embara Park, to see and be
seen, to trade in productions, to talk and meet new
faces. Here were his roots, so he felt, however
tawdry and perverse it might have become. Such
encounters still had the power to energize him. And
besides—what did it matter, where the City was?
Here, it was real and vital and showed no signs of
going away.

Brasille Sobranamest was located toward the center
of the city, among larger structures, but tastefully
set. It resembled the outdoor cafés of long ago, with
an exterior partially roofed against the heat of day
and the chill of night by an extended arbor of
grapevines, fox grapes, a wild breed that produced
small, black, very tart grapes whose taste was
unsurpassed. Now they were past their peak, but yet
leafy and green. A low planter set off the pavilion
from the avenue, filled with an inner and an outer
planting, the inner being soft billows of English
boxwood and the outer being tiny-leaved yaupon
intermixed with Pfizer juniper, which had been

Entertainment 165

carefully trimmed into grotesque and contorted
oriental shapes. The junipers and the boxwoods lent
the soft evening air a subtle, foxy odor full of
exciting pungencies.

Cormen walked casually along the outside of the
planter, as if just passing by, turning in as if struck
by a sudden whim, the best possible way to enter
such a place. Looking about, he could see no overt
attention being paid to him, but he sensed, rather
than directly perceived, that nonetheless he had
already been spotted and was being evaluated. Here,
now, there was an air, a distinct sensation, of being
in the highest levels: gestures were refined and
subtle. One would not hear loud guffaws, or sudden
raucous brays of laughter. Clothing was plain and
unrevealing, but to a person it was uniformly
understated and quietly elegant. He was pleased to be
here—for it was, indeed, an entry into the highest
levels.

Some had arrived early, and others were quietly
helping with the arrangement of the refreshments.
Guests, of course, were expected to help out, since
there were no servants or waiters. At first, as he
looked, he could not recognize Nilufer out of the
assembly, but after a moment, he saw her chatting
animatedly with a small group. She had her back to
him, but soon she turned to leave and caught sight of
him.

Once again, Cormen reminded himself that Nilufer
remained stunning, a figure of commanding attention
at any gathering. Tonight, she wore a simple woven
gown of a darkish blue-aqua color, but beneath the

dark outer color a reflecting layer had been woven into the fabric, for the gown rippled about her body like flowing waters softly shimmering. It concealed everything—and nothing at all. Underneath the fabric, Nilufer's ripe body moved, swaying and gliding, and her wonderful long black hair fell over her shoulders in cascades, a waterfall of darkness. She came to him quickly, as if they had been separated for years, and embraced him warmly, so that he could feel the varying patterns of softness and hard muscle beneath the gown. Cormen returned the embrace, brushing his lips lightly on both her cheeks.

When Nilufer spoke, her entire body spoke in tune with her words; she said, in a low voice which she seemed barely able to restrain, "At last! You are here! I almost thought you weren't coming!"

"Of course I am here! You asked me, didn't you?"

Nilufer looked to the side, coyly. "You only came for Corymont and his friends." She punctuated her assertion with a pout.

"Oh, no."

"Then worse; only for Faero, the new girl you don't even know."

"No."

She turned her face back to him, on a level with his own, breathless. "Then you must tell me!"

"I came solely to be captivated by your matchless animal magnetism. Corymont Deghil? Some moping aesthete. And another girl? Nilufer, you are absolutely unique, and tonight especially so. You are gorgeous, do you understand? And these subtle citizens of the higher orders may not be accustomed to such things.''

She gave him another quick hug, pressing her breasts against him. ''You are a dear, always the one with exactly the right things to say. You know very well that I did not emerge from the House of Life yesterday, and that I am no longer the gawky girl who came out and who was all legs and with a flat chest like a boy's . . .''

''The legs remain, and as for the rest, let the change be praised!''

''No, no! But it is true, that you said that I might be too much for these—they are subtle ones, and that's a fact!'' She glanced down, along the curving lines of her voluptuous figure, luxuriant and ripe. ''I have seen some here, for a fact, that I'd wonder what they were—so you could hardly tell the men from the women.''

Cormen laughed and said, ''Never worry, Ni': I'm sure that the distinction can be determined and appreciated by those who are really interested.''

''Yes, they'll find a way.'' She paused and looked about. Then, ''And as we speak of finding a way, now you come along with me! First to meet Faero Sheftali, and then Corymont, that moping aesthete, and then some others, equally interesting. This is to be a good night for you and me—we must circulate and be seen! As we are new in this group, we might expect a better cred after tonight, that is, if we ourselves do not spend it first, ha, ha!''

Nilufer took Cormen's hand and led him toward the back of the pavilion, where a solitary girl was standing by one of the serving tables. At first glance, she seemed plain and unassuming, and was dressed similarly: a loose, full skirt, a flowered peasant blouse, her shoulders covered by a thin wool shawl. Thong sandals. She was nibbling absently at one of the tidbits and looked rather out of place.

Nilufer swirled up to the girl and stood beside her, announcing breathlessly, "Cormen Demir-Hisar, you meet Faero Sheftali, a newcomer to our city who would need a guide in the ways of our world." She added, to Faero, "This is Cormen. He is inventive and well-balanced, and I mean the double-entendre. One of my protégés."

Now Cormen took the second glance for which he was so well-known. And indeed was it worth the second look: seen closely, Faero was indeed a girl of remarkable, still, subtle beauty. She was somewhat shorter than Cormen and Nilufer, yet not small or petite. Her figure was slight, the lines of her body firm and slender. The skin was a soft pale amber, with darker shadings along the lines of her collarbones which suggested a recent suntan over a paler original color. She had a small mouth, thin-lipped, and a rather sharp nose that lent her face an intent, predatory look. Determined, but graceful and wellformed. Her hair fell artlessly to her neck, each strand fine, but the fall of her hair was heavy, a pale brown color. She had tied a flower in her hair, which seemed to catch something about her—something innocent, yet adventurous and gallant. She also seemed a bit older, more advanced than the typical recent emergee; late in adolescence, but she did have something of the tentative, questioning air of such a one. Cormen took her hand; it was cool and dry, small-boned but firm. She was, all things considered, possessed of an extraordinary natural beauty such as one seldom saw.

Before Cormen could speak, Nilufer interjected, "Stop! Now you know who you are, and you can have all evening to know each other further. You are already moonstruck, both of you! Stop it—you will turn to stone! And now I will borrow Cormen for the others—just for a bit!" And she tugged his arm as they set off for another group. But as they left, Cormen managed to look back at the girl, and she caught his eyes and looked at him in turn with what he thought was a glance of the same meaning and the same intensity. Yes. He would definitely return.

Nilufer circulated Cormen around, making certain that he met everyone who was anyone, including the redoubtable Corymont Deghil, with whom he had an interesting, if brief talk. They traded some call-codes for some pieces. And for the rest, it went much the same, but very well, so he thought.

A by-product of the evening's circulations was that Cormen was asked for his own request-code several times, and of course he complied. One would never know, of course, whether it was actually used or not. But all in all, it was a fine evening in a new group, especially one so restrictive as this one. Nilufer agreed, having herself entertained a considerable number of requests for her call-code, which seemed to allay her fears that she might be too much for the high-class

gentlemen and ladies of the Deghil circle. And at last
satisfied that Cormen was properly oriented and off
on his own, and had learned a decent number of
names, she released him to wander about as he would.

As soon as he could do so with the minimum of
flurry, Cormen moved off through the crowd, looking for the girl, Faero. After some searching, he
found her, talking with an older couple who seemed
to know each other well. Cormen joined in, after
some perfunctory introductions which they all soon
forgot, and soon the couple drifted away.

Cormen secured a flagon of Bernkasteler Riseling
for them from the dispenser, a pair of goblets, and
conducted the girl to a quiet corner of the pavilion
where they might talk more privately. She took the
wine he offered her, shyly, and he began first, seeing
that she seemed somewhat backward and reticent.

"I can't say I'd blame you for feeling a bit out of
water in this group . . . but thank you for waiting for
me. All those people . . . this was necessary, you
know."

She replied in a soft, but confident voice, "So
Nilufer told me. Did it go well?" Her voice was soft
and pleasant, but very clear.

"Yes. At least, I think so. The next few days
should show some evidence of it . . . all seems
well."

"I am glad that you decided to come."

"It should be I who said that."

She looked aside, shyly. "I thought I would need
to meet someone who was curious about things; I
want to do as well as I can . . ."

"You make a better compliment than Deghil asking for me, I think . . . and I will do what I can. It helps to have one show you things."

"Yes. Nilufer doesn't do much, herself, except herself; but she does do very well at that."

"She is well-known and moves about a lot. Tell me, is it true that you have not given out your number to anyone?"

"True. The idea seems strange to me, that someone should be your lover and yet you wouldn't know it."

"Not knowing—no experience at all, except that such events appear in the Periodic Accounting Register."

"She told me about that, at the least. Well, I can wait. Perhaps I won't hand it out at all."

"Double or nothing?"

She smiled, softly but knowingly. "Yes."

"But what would you do, for yourself?"

She looked coy for a second, then herself again. "Might not."

"What a thought! Hardly anyone denies themself the least thing, in requesting company. Only minding one's budget, of course. But then you would be with us far too short a time, and I would not get to know you nearly as well as I would like to. Every thirteen weeks PAR is summarized, and if you are below the line, showing negative . . . then . . . ."

"I know. Back to the House of Life."

"I hope you will not."

"Nilufer has done well so far in introducing us . . . ."

Cormen smiled, and said, "I hope that I will not change your mind about that."

"No, I imagine not. And now you must tell me something about the real things you can do with MEC, besides order lovers of your choice, and food and clothing."

Cormen chuckled. "You are knowledgeable about one part of it, at least. I dare not ask . . ."

Faero smiled broadly, exposing perfect, small teeth. "And I would not dare answer, for then you would know my innermost secrets and fantasies. I already know: we don't ask and we don't answer."

He nodded. "But there are many other things you can do."

"How do you find the index that tells you how to do them?"

"Easy? there isn't one."

"There isn't one?"

"Exactly. At least, not in MEC that I know of. Well, even considering Original Works alone, such a list would be impossibly long—its very size and complexity would deter one from using it. The numbers really are staggering. And then come the productions, which are built up from Originals, which has the effect of multiplying all the lists by each other. Incalculable." He thought for a moment. "In fact, I'll tell you that sometimes it is extremely difficult to actually reach on Original, which is necessary for the best work. Some of these productions have been redone so many times that it is a major piece of work to find the Original it is based on."

She stood, seeming a little confused. She said, "Tell me, then."

"People have their own pet indexing programs which they collect and trade. The lower-power ones are sold in shops and are, it goes without saying, hardly worth the trouble. These, anyway, are called Basic Lists. They are traded mostly, outside MEC, as it were, person to person, this for that. Tonight, for example, I obtained a reference for a Bruillov, a Russian painter of the nineteenth century. I traded a reference to Michael Whelan for it. One for one, of the same basic art form. And tomorrow, or maybe tonight, I'll have MEC make me up a catalog of his works, and then we'll see what we can do with it. I can reproduce Originals, and if no one has the code reserved for it, I can corner their production. Also, I can order Projections, which are things the artist might have done, could have done, but actually didn't. Here, Time is no barrier, either. You can put any artist in any time frame. Past of him or future. Of course, the number of Originals is limited—but the number of Projections is endless. Then, from the style of the painter, we can process to cinema by animation."

"MEC fills in the motion?"

"Yes. Now here is a word of caution from an old practicioner of making Projections: stay away from the best artists, because the best ones, run through MEC and animated, become so dazzling that they erase consciousness of the story line. This is called media-swamping. Beginners often do this—they select styles too intense for the material of the story itself. Beautiful, but too bright, as we say. Be subtle and wary. Balance counts for a lot, because balance is what causes people to subscribe to your work, often, again and again.''

"MEC takes the credit from the viewer, and posits it to the producer . . .''

"That's right. And of course the same sort of things can be done with other forms, music, drama, live film cinema, too . . . It works the same way. And then you also find Viewpoints, or events in Spacetime, and they get credited the same way, if no one has claimed them, and there are endless ones not yet found. Of course, the more famous ones already have claimants. You learn which coordinates give the best results, for what you want to do. There, I can help you get started. I won't give you all my secrets, but I'll give you enough to give you a start.''

Faero looked thoughtful for a moment. "I understand that this is something that people don't give away.''

"Well, yes, normally; we wouldn't give so much away casually.''

"Then . . . why?''

"I should want you to stay as long as you can.''

"No one has made that kind of offer yet, save you.''

"I can sense that you are different. Unique. I would want more than a call-code.'' It was indeed more than he had ever said to anyone he had met.

She digested this, and then said, "But I'd have to carry a notepad around all the time.''

"Of course. Everyone does. You work to find the

best of all, all the things that fit you best, so that others will use them, and so your future is assured."

"How much future?"

"As long as you can keep a positive balance on the PAR. Beyond that, time is pretty meaningless, not at all as in the views. They had so little time . . . but we don't age like *they* did, or at least so it seems. Much slower, apparently. Everybody gets their chance in thirteen-week increments. Somebody like Deghil . . . I don't know how long he's been out of the House of Life. He was here, much as he is now, when I arrived. He's a bit of an exception, but many last long times. Then we could know each other for a long time." The prospect seemed inviting, as with none he'd met before.

She asked, "And what if I did none of this?"

Cormen felt a dizzy coldness wash over him. "If you do nothing, at the end of your first thirteen weeks you would show a negative balance in PAR, and that would be all. You would not be anymore. It would be a loss to me to have that happen. Please don't, at least for me."

Faero touched his hand lightly, her hand cool and damp from the wineglass. "I will try because you ask it. And what good fortune I have had, to find someone so interested, from the very first! I will try to live up to it. I really will!"

Cormen breathed deeply. "I need to know a little more about you, to begin properly; tell me about yourself—what do you like? Did Nilufer show you anything?"

She paused for a moment, looking off into space,

musing. "She showed me how to request things, and
some of the formats, and she gave me some samples
to work with, using her number. She gave me some
things, too, but most of them didn't fit so well."
Here, she looked down and gestured shyly at her
modest figure. "And the few that did fit—I couldn't
wear them. They were much too . . . flamboyant.
She is really a good person, she has a heart of gold,
really, but she is much too extroverted, too exotic."
She indicated her own modest clothing, which accen-
tuated her remarkable subtle, still, clear beauty.
"Something is missing, and Nilufer doesn't seem to
have the key."

"Music?"

"She always works dancing music; it's exciting at
first, but then . . . there seems to be no depth to it,
no . . . vision. I don't know."

"Projected stories?"

"All the things she showed me were either light
comedy or involved romances, emotional but not
really dramatic. She makes up a lot of them, constantly,
because not many reorder them."

Cormen nodded. He understood exactly. He retrieved his notebook, and, removing a sheet, wrote a
list on it and handed it to her. He waited for her to
look it over, and then said, "The first part are guides
on Search and Command subassemblies, and how to
get summaries. You have to limit them severely in
Time, Space and place, and be as specific as you can
be, because even with the limits that are, there really
are too many Originals. The other part is a list of
some examples. Some are mine, others are by other

people. They have program notes, which are very instructive. Those—use them sparingly. They cost credit.''

Faero looked over the second list for a moment. ''Tell me.''

Cormen paused for a moment, as if to gather his thoughts on the subject, which by implication was large. He began, ''Projections in Music are called Metamusic, for example. They remain, however far extended, identifiable with the Original artist. You can use a general program, or run what is called a Splice, you pick a specific point in time and extend-project from there. Then MEC generates what has the highest probability of being for works. What is done then is to search out the best ''eras.'' The search is endless, of course. For example, Beethoven.'' He raised his finger didactically. ''As an Original, he composed only nine symphonies. But when you Project him forward in time, he produces generally pastoral pieces, rather mild and bland, throughout the remainder of the nineteenth century, until after the great European wars. After number thirty, something of the old Beethoven reappears, and the symphonies rapidly improve after that. Number thirty-two in D-flat diminished is truly astonishing.''

He added, ''But with the popular artists, the process is harder, because they use a less formal method. It's all the same to MEC—it uses pattern-recognition beyond what we can, but for us it's hard to find the right place to splice on. Often you have to splice from a particular work . . . MEC reproduces the same proportion of good and bad work, so that the fractional ratio remains constant. Jim Morrison is the best example of this. Singer-songwriter for a group called the Doors. Some of the stuff stands with the best; other pieces are weak and overwrought. Their best work is classical in the sense that it's timeless—you can't pick up the dating marks of an era from it. And then there was Pink Floyd. Try a projection of their work, *Sacco and Vanzetti*. It's a good introduction to their work, even though it's a Projection. The painters are Kuniko Craft, Jeff Jones, Kelly Freas, Albert Feldstein and Max Ginzburg. You can get small Original catalogues for free. They have good notes: use them. That other item, *'Cycle one 5/4,'* is not a work, so to speak, but a collection—a random and arbitrary selection of jazz pieces of varying length, all in 5/4 time by the Brubeck Quartet—you can order something like that by simply specifying the number of pieces you want to have. By the way, I will add that 5/4 time sounds extremely odd the first time you hear it; but it grows on you. There is also an enormous catalogue of Rock done in 9/8 time, which is very dynamic and disturbing emotionally—very commanding. Basically, what you have to do is find pieces that no one else has a claim on, and then popularize them yourself. Then you grow into more complicated assemblies, combinations. The more basic units that go into the final result, the greater the reward.''

Faero said, after a moment, ''This is enormous in scope . . . Give me an example, a complete Production.''

Cormen pulled his chin and said, ''Very well . . .

Dune, Frank Herbert. This was an Original novel. Then it's done as cinema, animation, 93 percent adherence to the original text. You can't use 100 percent, by the way. Style of animation stills from Spain Rodriguez, color. He was one of the Underground Comic artists, violent and bizarre. Motorcycle gangs. The music is by Lou Reed, circa 1974 + . The music and the art style emphasize an element of excessive violence which was present in the Original. Not for the squeamish, but altogether excellent and deservedly popular. Not one of mine, incidentally. It's an old one, the producer long since gone back to the House of Life, so it's free. You program it into your view-window. Do it when you have some time, because it takes about six hours to see it all.''

He paused, and continued, "Or *Lord of the Rings*, J.R.R. Tolkien, animation from N.C. Wyeth, music by Bo Hansson. There have been a lot of trials of *Lord of the Rings*, but that particular one seems to be among the best I've seen.''

She said, "I see. You listed those, here. I have . . .''

"A lot to do.''

She looked at Cormen, bravely. "I will start . . . tonight.''

Cormen was silent for a long time, looking at her, the clear lines of her face. He said, "You know, of course, how to request the companionship of persons toward whom one feels love, desire, affection?''

Faero again looked coy and sly. "Of course.''

"It is considered desirable that people who meet and strike a responsive chord exchange their call-codes.''

"I understand that. Nilufer gave me yours."

"Could we do this?"

"Let it be different with us . . . I mean that we could do something unconventional and extraordinary: we could see each other in person."

She had said it in a normal tone, with no emphasis. But Cormen looked owlishly at her until she started giggling at his too-sober expression, and he realized how foolish he must look. He looked away, then back to her, and asked, "Are you serious?"

"Of course." She smiled, engagingly, warmly. "I think you are very nice. Why shouldn't I wish to see you?"

"But nobody does it that way!"

Faero asked, impudently, impishly, "Is there a rule against it? Will we be punished?"

"No rule, no law, no punishment. But everyone uses MEC; it has removed all the pretenses of the old times. What we now do with it is what people always really wanted . . ."

"Ha . . . And so you are the famous citizen who floated *The King in Yellow* out into the world, most recently, which has everyone gasping at its subtle horrors, when the prevailing fashion is eather maudlin soap operas, or else raw power-violence and even more impossible barbarians? And are you the Cormen who is preparing to resurrect Robinson Jeffers from the Centuries with a baroque, theatrical Rock band?"

"Who told you? Nilufer?"

"Indeed, who else? But you have an unconventional streak in you. And I have few habits in the life I now lead. I asked, and she gave you to me; she is terribly fond of you, and wishes you happiness in all things, and so I thought that we could do something different, while I learn.''

Cormen admitted to himself that she was indeed bold and gallant, to go so far. But that, in itself, did not seem a vice. She was quick and alert, and he felt that she was definitely a cut above the usual neophytes one met prowling about Embara Park, and other public meeting places. The idea intrigued him, and he said, "All right, Faero. We will not exchange numbers. When do we start?"

She shifted her mood, again, now sliding imperceptibly into a pensive, distant state. As if thinking aloud, she said, "You said that people got what they really wanted . . . I have an idea, that with all the traffic in the arts that we have, and in the sweet gluttony of the senses, all that is not what we really want, but that we miss the uncertainties, the anticipations, and yes, even the disappointments and pain.''

"And so you think that we search for it in the arts, in our Productions.''

"Perhaps . . ." She shifted again, becoming a little brighter. "But tomorrow I must do my work stint.''

"I also, by chance.''

She said, coyly, "Can we meet, tomorrow evening, here?"

"That can be done. I will.'' He felt lighthearted. "And then we will start.'' Cormen reached for a piece of cake on the tray, but as he bit into it, a small crumb caught at the corner of his mouth. Before he could brush it away, Faero stepped close, and took

the crumb with her lips. Cormen felt a warm, nibbling sensation, and a sudden hot flash along his
spine; it was an intimacy he had not imagined. She
stepped away, her eyes shining recklessly with mischief and delight, saying nothing. *But the message
was clear enough,* he thought.

After that, by common consent, they began to
circulate about, sometimes talking to each other, sometimes to others. During this time, he mentioned to
her the problem that he had been working on; he
thought she had asked about it. It was no matter, for
she could have easily heard of it from Nilufer, or
others, for it certainly was no secret. But shortly
after, while he was talking to some interested people
about *Roan Stallion*, she whispered in his ear that it
was late and she would have to go. They broke away
from the group, and went aside for the moment.

She said, "I ask you one thing before we part
tonight, a small promise that we shall make to each
other."

"I will listen; go on."

"Do not call for my Simula with the headset; I
will not call for yours."

"Why?"

"That we should be surprises to each other, is all;
I would know it if you did, and would never see you
again."

"How could you know?"

"I could see it in your eyes when you came to
me—you would know me, but I would not know you
in the same way."

"Oh, yes, I see. Very well—so it will be. But I

hope that you will take it as a compliment that I asked."

"I do. But there will be better. And now, good night, until tomorrow." And she took his face in her hands and kissed him, quickly, lightly, as one would kiss a child. A quick brush of her face against his, the scent of her hair, and she was gone into the night, to wherever she lived. Cormen realized then that he did not know where she lived. But of course there was tomorrow, as improbable as that seemed to him.

Before the evening came to a close, *Roan Stallion* was well on the way.

Back in his own house, Cormen undressed and prepared for bed, putting on his favorite bathrobe. He settled in the main room in his favorite chair. *Everest by Moonlight* was on the view-window, and the rest of the lights were off. That one was one of his own viewpoints, so it cost him nothing to use it. He watched the image of the mountain, and thought about this most curious evening, and the one girl who had made it so. Odd, that one, but tantalizing. Delicious. He continued to watch the image of the mountain in the window, following with his eyes the billowing of the snow-plume off the peak of the blue-black mountain mass. The speakers concealed in the walls faithfully reproduced the roaring of the icy winds that blow above 8,000 meters along the blind slopes of the highest mountain in the world . . . or whatever world it was they saw displayed in the viewpoints. But that was the other part of his Problem, and that part he kept strictly private, though it both-

ered him most of all: all that they all saw in the
views, everything—the vast armies, the great pulsing,
festering cities into which a score of their own tidy
little Cities might be dropped without a trace, the
lunging, charging machines. . . . And here, in the
world they walked and ate, and lived on, there was
no trace whatsoever of those energies, those artifacts,
those millions of lives, billions. No aircraft streaked
the sunsets along their quiet sea with vapor trails, no
ships plied the seas. Nobody came to visit. Nobody
left either, but somehow that seemed easier to explain.
He knew very well why no one left: everyone had
everything. What could there possibly be to leave
for? Yes, everything. Everything but a direct connection to the things that they saw on their viewscreens.
Cormen, in his searches, had often happened across
science-fiction stories, and there were aspects of this
that had that speculative ring to them. Perhaps they
were a forgotten colony somewhere, waiting . . . But
for what?

He got up and walked about the main-room uneasily,
nervously. This train of thought always bothered him,
for there seemed to be no hard answers in it, no
matter how hard or deeply he looked into it. Others
sensed it, he knew, but they carefully avoided even
asking the question. It was uncomfortable. So, those
billions in the viewpoints, in Time. Where were
they? *When* were they? And wherever they were,
where was he?

Cormen had a cure for too much of this. He went
to the bookshelf, where he kept his references, his
careful compilations that enabled him to make up the

Productions for which he was becoming so well-known. Among the volumes there would be one book, a listing of the call-codes of a number of girls. Many of them, doubtless, were absent, gone back to the House of Life, but called up by MEC in Simula they remained as fresh and as lovely as the first time he had met them. Holding the volume, he hesitated for a moment, thinking of Faero, and her simple, unadorned loveliness, her slight, supple figure, the warm tone of her skin, her charming expressions and gestures, her sense of intimacy. And he remembered his promise. Very well, that was, and he kept his word, but now he also wished for company, and the nepenthe of a warm body, too. He glanced at the tracking heatset, but he opened the call-code book and began leafing through it, with the ease of one familiar with the pages.

Inside, there was a page to each subject, showing a portrait, and a series of descriptive remarks, which were as often as not, acrid and cynical. Most of the description was not of faces or bodies—he knew them well enough—but of psyches and personalities, the innermost of them. This one: Kerim Kavaklidere, K-10019. It said, after a bit of physical overview . . . "Difficult and bitchy; intense, opinionated and athletic. Inventive and high-strung, likes to argue politics, although specific ideology may shift." Cormen smiled at the description. Acrid but accurate. He remembered the call-code number. He replaced the book in the bookshelf in the darkened room and dialed in the number in the request console: K-10019. Kerim would do. She would clear his head, and purge his soul; she was good for that. Cormen returned to his chair, and sat down to wait.

Some came early, some came late; some came casually, some came running, breathless. One could never be sure with Kerim.

Time passed, and then a little more. She was late this time. Cormen shivered a little, thinking, *When she's late, she's wild; may even want to argue first, over something absurd, like who's on top, first. One never knows.*

The bell for the door chimed softly, and Cormen got up, and went to it, opening it. On the doorstep stood a tall, thin girl with an angular, but interesting face, and long, straight blonde hair. She said, without pleasure, ''Do I have to stand out here all night? It's damn cool out here!''

He opened the door farther and let her in. Kerim strode into the room as if it were hers and looked about as if she expected to find something repulsive lying on the rug. Finding nothing, she looked at the dimmed lighting, and at the view-window, at the mountain visible there. She placed her thin arms on her hips and stared at the picture for a time, and then turned to Cormen: ''Here it is autumn outside, damp and chilly at night, and you have snow at your window, hurricanes! Do you know how impossible you are?'' She wore a thin silk shift which left her arms bare.

''It's just a picture: we can change it. What would you like?''

'Something hot! I really am chilled to the bone. Be a dear and order something hot, please.''

"Something jungly?"

"Ugh! Brightly colored disgusting creatures full of parasites!" Kerim was as lean and nervous as a starved panther. She had a long, intense face full features, and in some lights there was a definite suggestion of equine lines there—indeed, she hovered on the line between uncompromising homeliness and remarkable beauty. She pursed her lips and added, "Really, Cormen, you always keep the same visuals on the wall like the tabards of some moribund dynasty." Her voice was penetrating and nasal, but totally without whine. "And Constantine Yuon pencil drawings! Academic Formalism! I suppose you have a Modigliani nude in the bedroom!"

Cormen answered mildly, "Why no, as a fact, although I do have a Salomé of unsurpassing wantonness, done by Frank Frazetta, and also a very wild thing called 'The Apotheosis of Jimmy Carter' by Abdul Mati Klarwein. He's the one that does those surrealistic murals that look like Hindu temple scenes— blue-skinned goddesses, monkey gods, all that. All sorts of wanton women."

She looked interested, for a change. "Really? A Klarwein? Now this might be interesting, after all. Cormen, you take on luster! And of course Salomés are always entertaining . . ." Here she leered at Cormen, wickedly, caricaturing lust and producing an image of anger, or frustration. She continued, "Well! I have an urge to be a desert woman! A Delilah, a Zenobia, a Sheba."

Cormen laughed. "Judith was also a desert woman,

but she took the head of the great general, Holofernes, for her people.''

Kerim shook her head. "No heads, and I won't cut your hair." She turned, spun about as if dancing, stepped, glided, and made a short leap that looked much longer, a motion of surprising grace. Perhaps the Original-in-Time Kerim was based on had been a real dancer. She added, "I might perform a lewd dance, just to warm up!"

Cormen nodded and turned away for a moment, to dial in a change into the view-window controls. Mount Everest faded, darkened, went out. Darkness. The window cleared again, to: a desert of rock and sand. In the distance were eroded buttes, outcrops, stark empty mountains, a desolation. In the middle distance the ruins of a city could be seen, its columns and porticos and avenues sharply etched in the reddened light of a low sun. The slender columns were abandoned and eroded by time and fortune. There was a sensation of dull heat through the window.

Kerim glided to the window-wall and gazed thoughtfully into the distances, slowly relaxing as she luxuriated in the light and heat. She said, softly, now. "This is very good, Cormen. Tell me what it is. It is better than I expected of you."

"Persepolis, an evening in August in the year 710 AD. At the time you see here these ruins were a bit more than a thousand years old—unspoiled by nomads, who fear the place. Also unspoiled by tourists. I have other desert scenes, but this one I especially like."

Kerim relaxed, visibly, facing the window, letting her thin shoulders sag, turning her face up slightly,

tensing the tendons in her fine, graceful neck. Then
she stretched, inhaling deeply, reaching for the ceiling with her fingertips: she could almost touch it.
Letting her arms fall, she sighed, an oddly peaceful
sound for one usually so combative and argumentative.
Cormen joined her before the view of the desert,
stood close beside her, half facing her. He touched a
strand of the silky find pale hair falling past her ear,
stroked it lightly. Kerim continued to gaze into the
distance, but the hard, intense focus of her eyes
faded, and she looked pensive, and a little sad. He
could sense the warmth of her body through the thin
dress she wore. He touched the shell of her ear,
tracing the line of it, her temples; he brushed the
backs of his fingers along her cheek, the line of her
jaw. She relaxed, tilting her head back. Cormen
traced with his fingertips the outlines of her nose, her
lips, and Kerim reached for his face with hot hands
and turned to him, eyes bright and lustrous and
all-seeing.

When Cormen awoke in the morning, he felt stiff and
groggy, and for some time did not move. No one was
with him in the bed, as he expected, although there
was in the air, in the bed, a slightest trace of the
pungent, aromatic scent Kerim used. He reflected,
yes, this was the right way, the old way, the way we
all knew. Not that Faero wasn't something special—
she certainly was—but he felt as if he had re-
emphasized his personal sense of identity, reality.
True: Faero was something out of the ordinary. As a
fact, she was fascinating. But it was equally true that

his life had been composed of incidents like this, with Kerim, with Nilufer, with others too numerous to name; they shaped him, tuned him, and delineated his identity.

From the other room, his musings were interrupted by the soft chime of an incoming call. Struggling with bedcovers that suddenly seemed uncooperative and tangled, he made his way from the bed into the main room, to face the elliptical communicator, running his fingers through his hair. He straightened his robe, and waved his hand before the mirror. The mirror went dull, smoky, and then cleared.

Cormen recognized the caller: it was Corymont Deghil. Deghil was thin and aristocratic in manner, at once conveying the impression of effortless languour combined with a microscopic precision of thought. Gray hair showed at his temples, and his face, sharp-featured and hawklike was as impassive as that of an idol.

Deghil began, "Please forgive my rudeness and accept my apologies: I always assume that everyone lives as I do, up at dawn. It was not my intent to awaken you. But I recalled that you mentioned that you had a duty-day today, I believe."

Cormen answered, "No matter, there. I was awake, indulging in the recollection of a late revel. I should be getting on my way shortly."

Deghil smiled and said, "Exactly so! Of course, all must strive a little, all the same I endeavor to forget mine as much as it is possible to forget anything. I dimly recall that on certain days, I have something to do with the lubrication of unspecified machineries.

And I believe that I have heard that you have the honor of performing quality assurance at the main flow nexus of the Division of Nutriment.''

"That is so, impossible as it seems on days like today.''

Deghil continued, "Thus—I will be on to the matter. I wished to convey my appreciation, as well as those of our little association, for the insights you provided us at Brasille Sobranamest. Indeed, much of last night was spent in evaluating, weighing fine points, and the verdict is unanimous: *Roan Stallion* performed by Genesis is a production of surprisingly superior merit. I know the Originals well, and was pleasantly surprised by the combination. They turned out to be rather more musical and less loud than the usual practitioners of the form—but equally startling. I trust you have reserved the remainder of Jeffers— else I would claim them myself.''

"I have claimed them for this combination, but there are still details to be worked out before I release others.''

"Excellent! We plan to have another gathering of our circle and wish to extend our invitation . . . and of course, bring your most prized Productions with you. You have a sure touch for it, my boy, and I feel certain that this will mark the beginning of a long and profitable association for us all. Day after tomorrow, at Sofiya Sobranamest. I might add, this will be a special meet, not so many folk there and so we can be . . . ah, more ourselves, there's the word.''

"You may rely on me; I will be there.''

"Who was the girl you spent the evening with?

But never mind—surprise me. But bring her, too."

"That seems possible, although I must say that she is a bit shy about her call-code, that much I can tell."

"No matter, no matter. Ha, ha. We have our ways around such reticence, don't we? And for now, then, good day." The image faded, went opaque, and the mirror was just a mirror again.

Cormen began pacing about the living room, suddenly awake with fresh excitement and plans. The long project had worked! The preparation, the study, the research, the cunning slow buildup by Nilufer, among others, all had finally worked. Now he was in the highest circles. All he had to do was to mind his manners and keep his ears open, and a long lifeline was assured. There would be plenty of time, now, to attack and unravel all those problems in which he had maintained a secret indulgence all these years. And of course, his Problem . . . But in this new light, the Problem seemed to have lost some of its edge—not so important anymore, somehow. Cormen stopped and smiled to himself: it might be possible to ignore it entirely. Perspectives changed with circumstances.

He headed for the kitchenette to program a breakfast, but on the way something caught his eye, lying in the message tray attached to the mainframe console. A long printout. He stopped and stared at it with a sinking feeling of fear and apprehension. No! Not now, so close! He recalled with the same sinking feeling that it was time for his Period Accounting Register to arrive. He had utterly forgotten about it. He swallowed, hesitating to even touch it. And he found himself wondering, just how was one called back to the House of Life? Did they know? Were they called upon by assassins? Was there fear? Pain? He had heard rumors that there was neither. Yet he did not wish to find the solution to that mystery; it could wait, indefinitely.

Cormen reluctantly picked up the PAR; it showed the final summation on the top line, and so he read on with a lightened heart: $+42170$. He was, as of this morning's sunrise 42,170 units ahead. Safety, safety, and a good increase over the last register. Nevertheless, he stopped now and read carefully through the category listings included in the register, observing which areas were strong, and which ones were weak. All seemed reasonably well-balanced; although "Real-Life Adventure Narratives" seemed especially weak. It was an area, he knew, that he would have to bring up to speed. That fitted in well with some plans he had been working on: he had tentatively titled it, *The Circumnavigation of Antarctica in a 7-Meter Sailboat*, by Robert Pirsig, Ken Kesey, and Hunter S. Thompson. Of course, he was certain that they hadn't actually done it, although they were contemporaries. But that was a trifling detail which MEC could resolve. What was crucial here was the blended style with which such an adventure might be portrayed, and how each contributed to the final work: the Gonzo madness of Thompson, the earthy pungency of Kesey, and the lucid sanity of Pirsig.

In the area discreetly entitled "Erotic Diversions," his credit side reflected a healthy number of requests,

and oddly, especially so in the doubled rate of blind,
one-time calls. There was no way to determine, of
course, by whom the calls had been made. But however it was, it seemed that he had some admirers
somewhere. Well enough!

In a more expansive mood, now, he considered the
register of his own requests, which were quite specific in names and dates and numbers. He knew
already, but was pleased to see reflected in print the
fact that he had restrained his impulses to select his
partners from the ranks of random passersby, as many
did. No headset calls in this period! There were
twenty-nine items billed to his account, and he noted
with some fond recollection that Nilufer's name occurred five times, and that his most recent adventure
with Kerim had also been dutifully recorded. He
smiled at that, and at the recollection of those times
with Nilufer. There was nothing in her appearance
that belied her performance and manner in more
intimate encounters. He glanced again at the list,
smiling absently, and then frowned, looking back
sharply at the list, particularly the last five items:

R25: Emeksiz, Nilufer.E77092/818 . .DB100
R26: Pervane, Kim.P44699/822 . . . . .DB100
R27: Velet, Palisandre.V31225/828 . .DB100
R28: Ariamne, Lunette.A82150/902. .DB100
R29: Kavaklidere, Kerim. K10019/910 DB:NC

There was no billing for Kerim. This could only
mean that she had already returned to the House of
Life. Persons so designated were carried as a no-
charge item for requests during the PAR period of

thirteen weeks after their Redline Report. After that, their request number was voided and double-billing was used, with one-time request codes furnished by MEC.

Of course, it was true that he hadn't seen her for some time, in person . . . but it gave him a momentary sense of chill, almost a shiver, to think of it: it was almost as if he had made love with a ghost.

Cormen thought the news sufficiently disturbing to have it confirmed with Nilufer, who would have an idea from the talk she always kept up with. And it would be good to speak with her, too, for this was a circumstance Cormen could not recall experiencing before so directly. He felt empty and sad: with all her flaws, Kerim had meant something to him, once. He felt a little guilty—perhaps he could have requested her call-code more, in place of, say, Kim, or Lunette, or some of the times with Nilufer.

Cormen dialed the number for communication, and expectantly waited for the screen to clear. There was no doubt that she'd be in. Nilufer was a late sleeper; and however many beds her Simula cavorted in last night in the throes of love, the Prime Nilufer was at home in her own bed.

The mirror trembled and faded, but did not clear. Instead, the mirror stabilized to a dull gray and the following legend appeared on it:

THIS NUMBER IS NO LONGER IN SER-VICE— PLEASE CONSULT YOUR DIREC-TORY FOR APPROPRIATE ACTION OF COR-RECTION AND/OR DELETION.

The letters faded as they had come, gradually. At a moment in which Cormen could not be sure that they was completely gone, the screen trembled, and became a mirror once again.

He stared at the mirror, seeing only his own rumpled reflection in it. He was completely at a loss for any action. This was insane: of course Nilufer was in. She was always in, in the mornings. And there never was a malfunction.

Cormen turned to the request console, approaching it warily, and dialed in a request for Nilufer Emeksiz, E77092. There was a way to test this, something he hoped most fervently wasn't so. The receipt light illuminated, then went out. Pulling the keyboard out of its slot, he typed in, EFFECTIVE IMMEDIATELY. He waited a moment, and then sent, CANCEL PREVIOUS REQUEST. ACKNOWLEDGE VALID BILLING. He waited another moment, and then sent, TRANSMIT CREDIT SUMMARY OF LAST REQUEST FOR E77092.

He stood back, sliding the keyboard back into its slot. Then he waited. After a moment, a small piece of paper slid out of the message slot and into the receptacle. He picked it up, noticing a slight trembling in his hand as he did so. It read.:

R01: Emeksiz, Nilufer. E77092/911......DB:NC

He forced himself to think rationally. A cancel after a request for immediate service was charged in full, without exception. It was just as if she had come. And the paper in his hand, now, said it: No

Charge. Nilufer Emeksiz, E77092, properly speaking, did not exist anymore.

Toward the end of the day, Cormen emerged from the Nutriment Distribution Center into the magic fading light of evening. There had been a transient hot spell during the day, which now the buildings and pavements gave back, putting out a glossy warmth against the cooler evening airs. But the air from the sea was fragrant and cool and bracing. He considered retiring early, perhaps with a trial-text of the Real-Life Adventure he was working on—*Antarctica*/Pirsig, Kesey, and Thompson. Cormen always faced his assignments squarely. He had the parameters for the basic text already drawn up, and it seemed ready enough, at least for a check. His ultimate plan was to make it into a narrated cinema account, with some music in parts, most probably something from the works of Anton Bruckner. But the narrator was still a problem. He would have a better idea after he had seen the first trial-text.

At the foot of the broad flow of marble stairs down from the building, the way was guarded by a pair of winged horses, the product of someone's private project long ago, for to his knowledge they had always been there. And that struck him as odd, because so little of what they did through MEC left behind artifacts as solid as the winged horses, each one apparently carved out of a massive, flawless block of blue granite. The horses were slightly larger than life-size, and the spread wings, as if poised for an immediate flight, were, in their turn, equally impres-

sive. Immense. And sitting by the hooves of the one
on the left, Faero waited, childlike and innocent, her
face illuminating in a warm smile when she caught
sight of him coming down the stairs.

This evening, she wore a gauze blouse, off-white,
and a brown, loose skirt which fell to her knees,
leaving her brown legs bare. On her feet were light
leather thong sandals. She sprang to her feet, and
skipped up the stairs to meet him, full of animation
and gaiety. Cormen took the hands she offered, touching his cheek to hers. "This is a fine surprise! I was
going to wait for your call; I would not have expected that you'd come in person!"

She looked down, blushing. "I know that I left too
soon last night, without leaving you a way to call
me. I was rude. So, since it was I who insisted on
real contact, I thought this might be the best way."

He said, "I am glad you came—you are a wel-
come sight after a dull workday."

"I had one too." She laughed.

"Did you! I never asked what you did on your
workdays."

She said, proudly, "I am a technician of the Master Memory Section." After she said it, an odd grimace flickered across her face, as if she regretted
having said it.

Cormen's eyebrows rose. "By now you must know
that this is a most extraordinary position. That is a
restricted area."

Faero said, thoughtfully, "And so it is. Perhaps in
where I go. Yes—yet what I do there seems ordinary
enough: repairs and checks. Someone has to crawl in

there and inspect, remove things, clean corrosion. I know that the position is not exercises all the time, but just every so often, as needed, so it seems.''

Cormen asked, mock-incredulously, ''Oh, is there much wrong, in there?''

Faero laughed her marvelous clear laugh, full of bubbling mischief, and exclaimed, ''Yes, yes! Oh, MEC is well into incipient senility.''

He frowned. ''Not so! My mainframe was prompt enough about billing me!''

She laughed again, ''That will be the last section to fail!'' Then she added, more seriously, ''Not so . . . There is remarkably little wrong inside, and so my work is as tedious and exiguous as anyone else's. Still, it needs doing, I suppose, else I would not be here.''

Cormen smiled warmly. ''Praise the requirement, otherwise we would not have met.''

She looked knowingly at him, as if they already shared a deep secret. ''We would have found a way, don't you believe that?''

''Possibly. I would have hoped so. And now— how are you progressing with your studies?''

She answered, ''I stayed up late last night, working on it, I did, Cormen, and I have some tentative things, but I can't say if they are worth viewing or not.''

''Nonsense! You have to start somewhere; how would you learn, otherwise?''

''So I thought last night . . . But today . . . I found out immediately that what you had warned me about, about lists, was true; when I didn't restrict the categories in either time or substance, the MEC would send me a funny little word on the screen: *Googol*. Then it would start transmitting the lists.''

"*Googol* means a very large number, not infinite, but indefinitely large. What did you do?''

"I would stop it. And then start over, after limiting. But you miss so much!''

"I know.''

"But more by accident than by any other way, I did find some things, and put a little bit together. And now you can tell me what I have done—rightly or wrongly.''

"Where shall we view this?''

"At my house, of course.''

"Lead the way—I will do my best.''

"You are kind to a newcomer—perhaps you are to be more strict as a teacher.''

"Not so. Every student needs some warmth and encouragement, too.''

She smiled, lazily, as if she were reading his mind and found it agreeable. "Yes, that. Yes, so far, I have missed that, as well. That is a disadvantage of meeting this way. And so, then. To my house.''

"I wonder why we did not go before; last night.''

"I still had some rearranging to do. It was recently inhabited, and the former tenant left behind much that was hers; I still haven't gotten rid of all of it.''

"Hers?"

"Yes, I think so, although I am only guessing. But I wanted you to see me reflected there when you came, for we are the only people in the wide world doing this, this way, you know.''

"Ah! I suspected that much, at any rate!"

As they walked now, she looked deeply at him, eyes enormous, all pupil. "Yes, tonight! We will play games and tease one another!"

"You are an incurable romantic."

She looked off, in the direction of the sea, to the south, and quoted:

> "What other consolation remains us than wine,
>   And three nights' moonlight on the Bosphorus divine?"

Then, after a moment, she added, apparently in the original language of the lines:

> "Ne kaldi ruha teselli Sharabdan bashka
>   Boghaz'da üch gejelik mahtabdan bashka."

Cormen asked, "And wherever did you find *that*?"

Faero skipped ahead, and looked back over her shoulder, coyly, letting the loose neck slip to expose one smooth shoulder. "It was Yahya Kemal Bayatli, early century twenty, Turkish. He was a poet. I had it translated. I found it in another context. It's marvelous in the original language, isn't it?"

"That was Turkish?"

"Yes. It's always correct to mumble in Turkish. Makes it sound right."

"And how did you arrive at Istanbul and early twentieth-century Turkish poets?"

"That takes a lot longer to tell than it took to do, I can tell you that! But it *was* lovely, just as Bayatli said it was. There was a soft light to the city—it was always so."

"Always?" For a moment, Cormen did not follow her thought at all."

She corrected, "Whatever date I selected. The shape of the city changed, but never the quality of the light." She changed the subject. "But now let us talk together and just be us. We will pass the people at their pleasures, their desires, their entertainments. It is evenings, and the sobrany begin, and all the informal meetings in the parks and plazas. To see, and to be seen!" Her eyes sparkled for a minute, and then faded a little. She said, "Come with me: I would that we walked together by the sea. And then I will show you."

Cormen offered her his arm. "Lead on—it is your evening."

By the time they had reached the suburbs adjacent to the sea, it was near dark; far off in the west, there remained a luminous indigo glow in the sky, but to the southeast, over the palm-fringed islands far out in the bay, the stars were out, even near the horizon. There was a soft, sea-fragrant breeze, and small, lazy waves stroked the beach sands without sound. Faero had removed her sandals and carried them, wading in and out of the water. Behind them on the shore, a few houses, in stucco, red tile roofs, and gray-weathered wood, climbed a sandy rise back to the city, hidden among palms, zamias, and fragrant groves of chamaecyparis, incense cedar, and ilex.

They had kept a silence between them on the way. But at last breaking the mood, Cormen ventured, "I thought that you were full of joy and enthusiasm, back there. But here, you are subdued and somber."

"Try as I will, I cannot rid my mind of thoughts . . .
I have not been able to find Nilufer, and her house is
empty."

"You know where it is?"

"Yes. She found me wandering when I came out;
and took me to her own place until I could find my
own. But she was very troubled: she thought she had
problems with the Periodic Accounting Register. She
told me some things to avoid, so as to miss excessive
charges. I know no more. But, Cormen, I think she
was called back to the House of Life, and I feel a
melancholy spirit in me, because you and Nilufer
were, are, the only people I know at all, and I would
lose neither of you. It makes me worry, that is all."

He said, "No need to worry about me—my PAR
is good. But I also know that Nilufer is missing. This
morning I tried to call her, but the number was
shown as invalidated. I thought I knew her well
enough—we have been friends for years, but she
never mentioned that she was worried about her
balance. And even so, I knew very little about what
she did herself. I suppose we hardly knew each other
at all."

"That was why I asked you to meet with me in
person, and not through Simulas."

"Perhaps you might be right in this, although it
would set a novel precedent, you know."

"I will not worry—except about those trips you
make along the edges of the city."

He looked up, suddenly. "I don't make that many

of them, anymore . . . How do you know about them?''

"She told me, Nilufer. Knowing that gives me an anxiety for you—prowling the edges, actually going outside the city. How far out have you gone, Cormen?''

For a moment, Cormen felt an uncertain and alien element present in this girl who seemed, most of the time, to be all charm and surprises. The questions fell naturally, and were voiced in the mildest of manners, but behind them was an edge of something he could neither see nor comprehend. Still, he could find no fault in answering them, because for all that they were still valid questions. "I'd say for the most part, they were short excursions of at best no more than a few hours' duration—in sight of the city. Once, mind you, I crossed the river—it's shallow and full of gravel on the bottom—and walked a whole day eastward, and actually spent the night in the open, camping. Roughing it.''

Faero placed her fingertips to her lips and her eyes grew round. She exclaimed, "What did you see?'' She added, "You fool, you might have been eaten by some wild thing!''

Cormen reassured her. "Nothing! There simply was nothing. Some small animals, the natural noises of birds and insects—and as far as I could see, the experience was disappointing. At least I could understand why no one goes to the east. Who knows how far the dunes extend?''

Faero added, slyly, "You could have used the

Views, set in the City-Now mode; it would have been slow, but far less dangerous.''

"It is slow and tedious; and I could see for myself that there was nothing there. The land is empty . . . just wilderness. I don't understand this, but at least I can accept it as a fact.''

Faero seemed to relax, and dragged her feet in the water, making pleasant splashing sounds. "It didn't whet your curiosity?''

"It did, then. It took me a long time to see it—what was the question I was supposed to ask, of all that: not, 'Where are the others?' but, 'Why are there no others?' I never found the answer . . . But anyway, it all has shifted priorities now, and doesn't seem to matter very much anymore.''

She stopped, and looked directly at him. "How so? I know you to be deep, deep into mysteries which others do not even know exist—or care.''

He said, "Thanks to Nilufer's aid, I was able to enter Deghil's circle. and that process was complete at the Sobrana at which you and I met. An omen, if you will. I arrived, and met you. Nothing could be clearer to me, and thus there is change and development. I am in the place I have worked to be in, and so for the moment, the old private project can be put aside—perhaps indefinitely, for I will really have to dig hard, now. So, I foresee no more trips outside for some time . . . maybe never.''

"Are you serious?'' Cormen could not help but note an element of agitation, even alarm, but he could not see why, and so he ignored it.

He stopped walking, considered, and then answered

carefully, "The great freedom of being a nobody is that you can do as you please. But when you have become part of desirable and influential circles within the world you have, then you pay a certain price. I saw it coming with open eyes and few illusions, and agreed to pay it. I chose this way, and now I will endeavor to fit in. Oh, I may look back and wonder— and it may color the way I make up my Productions, but all the same, I know what I must do . . . And I hope that this new direction would include you in it as well, no matter how unconventional you might seem now. You will go through the same changes I have; you have much promise." He added, "And Deghil asked that you come, too, tomorrow night, at Sofiya. You should, with this, be more than able to make it easily on your own, and I will do all I can."

Faero bent, wetting her hand, and dampened her face with the salt water. She said, "Is this truly the way?"

He answered, "That we help those we love and admire to join in the successes we find, as much as we can. What else can we offer in this world, which is the only one we have?"

"Indeed. I understand how priceless such a thing is . . . But you know me so little—how could you know if I would succeed as you have?"

Cormen shrugged. "I don't know, but I hope, from the evidence I can see, and . . ."

"Yes?"

". . . I would not have one I am becoming enchanted with, fond of, slip from me the way Nilufer did. She did all for me—I could have done for her—the same. But I assumed that she was fine, on her own, and so let her go on, and now . . ."

She turned to him suddenly and embraced him tightly, pressing wet kisses on his face, kisses that tasted of salt, a genuine expression of something, maybe desire, maybe something else. She stopped and turned away, concealing her face. Cormen turned so as to see her face, and saw that it was streaked and flushed, and that her eyes were wet and shiny. He asked. "Faero, what is it?"

She bent and splashed salt water on her face again and said, her voice unsteady, "Nothing, nothing. A passing fit, if you will. You have a strange effect on me . . . I suppose that is what we are. Or at any rate, soon will become."

Cormen ventured, "Lovers? In person, as Primes? Ah, now—there we enter a land none has walked for uncounted years."

She took his hand and came closer, brushing her lips against his as they walked. After a moment, she said, "Would Cormen the curious wonder how many years—how long that really is?"

"No. I would not have it otherwise, even though others did the same all around us."

She skipped a little dancing circle around him, spattering the warm water, and coming around to face him, she took both his hands in hers, squeezed them tightly, and then pressed them to her breasts, whispering, "Then we will go to my house now, and you will be my lover, yes, and I will be yours, yes, and the first time we lie together we will dedicate that to the memory of Nilufer."

"Yes. And then?"

"And then we must go as far as we can, for the world is a firefly shadow, the memory of a passing cloud; and we know only that we are here and now and that the real thing, the sweetness we will make with our bodies will be never again in this world."

"We are unique."

"Everyone is . . . but they don't realize it. We do, now."

She now walked gravely out of the water, as if reluctant to part from it, still holding Cormen's hands tightly, leading him away from the sea, toward the seaside gardens and cottages, the intangible neighborhood in which lay her house, somewhere. It was not far, only a few minutes' walking, which they now prolonged, sometimes stopping for a time to exchange light, teasing, tantalizing kisses, subtle, fleeting touches.

She led him into the garden of an inconspicuous house which evoked echoes in Cormen's mind, but he could not place them. Somewhere he had seen this house, this garden, but where? He couldn't place it; nor, with Faero teasing him as she was, could he manage to think clearly enough to make much of an effort to do so. Faero opened the door; inside, she left the lights off, leaving Cormen for a moment to program the View-wall. He waited, She tossed her sandals into the corner, unwinding her wraparound skirt, letting it fall off her hips. The view came on: a peaceful dusk by a country pond—a small pond with some clumps of cattails, bordered by tall pines whose branches were high overhead. The pond was glassy smooth, still; over its surface swallows darted, swooped, skimmed. A heron glided into view with its sinister measured gliding flight, dipped near the surface, dipped once to the surface with its beak, and flew on, rising slowly. To the left, there was a darkened cabin, old-fashioned and rustic, log walls and a screen porch. The sounds of night-things could be heard, crying off in the distance. The fading daylight in the View was soft and full of warm tones; in this light Cormen could see the smooth supple shape of her hip and thigh on the screen side of her as she came to him, and her skin was cool to the touch when he gathered her into his arms. Faero quite forgot to remove her thin blouse. In fact, it did not occur to either of them until much later. They also forgot to cry out in memory of Nilufer.

Much later, they returned to the sitting room (the pond was still on the View-wall), which also seemed to have some of the same strange familiarity Cormen had noticed in the garden outside. Familiar, yet strange. Faero scattered cushions on the floor and ordered, through the kitchen unit, bowls of fresh fruit, which she cut up for them using her own deft hands: apples, pears, tangerines, tart quinces, wild grapes almost black. There were also tart wild plums, apricots, wild cherries, wafers of cardamom oatmeal bread, and carafes of scented tea. They sat on the floor by a low taboret and said meaningless things, smiled at each other, and placed bits of fruit in each others' mouths.

During a quieter time when they were concentrating more on the tea, and on such thoughts as they

had, Faero retrieved the remote controller handset
from its slot in the wall and brought it back with her.
She settled herself, and said, "I want to show you at
least one of my inventions, to see what you think . . .
if we should present this to the regard of the worthy
Corymont Deghil and his friends, among whom is
you, now."

Cormen arranged his cushions and lay back, pulling a pale plaid lap-blanket over his slender frame,
relaxing. "Tell me first—what's it made up of?"

Faero moved her cushions so that they lay side by
side, and borrowed part of the blanket. She began,
"This will be animated cinema. I queried to see if it
had been done this way, and no one had before,
although the basic Original has been used often. The
base plot, the Original, is Shakespeare's *Romeo and
Juliet*, but instead of the Italianate background I set it
in a so-called "modern" style, very bare, with a lot
of pale surfaces and climbing plants. The presentation is full-animation, art by a popular artist named
Rosamond. She did a lot of subtle, lovely girls and
some unearthly children. The musical accompaniment is metamusic based on the early woodwind
compositions of Dmitri Shostakovich, and the words
are by Michael McClure and Diane Wakowski. There
was a feedback effect from the music, so that this
worked best at only about 80 percent reproduction of
the original text. Are you ready? I am very nervous
about this."

"Yes, yes! Do not lose your nerve now: run it!"

Faero keyed a coded sequence into the handset,
and the View-wall faded out the cabin scene and

replaced it, fading it in, with another scene, at once strange and disturbingly familiar: there were buildings of whitewashed stucco, vines trailing over walls, the sense of pale, filtered sunlight, and an odd, faded-out background. Somewhere off-screen was a pool which reflected light onto the wall, ripples and dancing patterns of half-shadows; bright lines of the rippling reflections pulsed and shimmered into the lettering of the titles and credits, and then this faded out, like a cloud passing over the sun, to the story itself. During this introduction, half-heard, there was a soft theme playing, the music made by a trio consisting of cor Anglais, tenor saxophone, and electric bass, at the lowest possible dynamic level, painfully tender but also with an undisguised undertone of pure slavonic melancholy.

Cormen said that he was already impressed, and he added, whispering, "Who are the musicians in this passage?"

Faero whispered quickly, "Yusef Lateef on cor Anglais: he was a jazz figure. Dick Parry on saxophone: he worked with group Pink Floyd, and Michael Rutherford on bass—an eight-string, by the way. Sh. Now watch and listen."

Unfolding now was a street scene in some city, a severely modern city, perfect and beautiful and spare, along which street two harlequin bullies were swaggering in mime, talking loudly and swearing most crudely, in complete defiance of their lovely environment. . . .

. . . And the last scene ended in a section given over to memorials to the dead of the city, the view closing in to focus on a single tear in the eye of the Prince, now zooming in close, close, picking up the refraction of the sun in the teardrop, glittering, while a fading saxophone played out the last fragments of melody and died out in its own echoes. With the silence, the reflections fell to the edges of the View-wall, and the wall became blank and pale. Then it went neutral.

Cormen took a deep breath and stretched. "I have been completely oblivious of the passage of time; of this piece, I need to say no more."

She asked softly, "You don't think it's too much? I mean . . ."

"I know what you mean. Well—it is extreme in its own way, but I also know a secret about art, that good art is an indefinable mix which lies on the border somewhere, between Harmony and Invention, and between 'good taste' and 'bad taste,' as it were. I like that spare scenery treatment very much—you could use that in a lot of ways, a lot of things. It's a long way toward an abstract kind of starkness, but also very lovely in execution . . . piercing. I would subscribe. Indeed I will. You are better than you know at this—and with so little time!"

"No, you must not subscribe. I will play it for you whenever you want. Let it be my gift to you; as with the Simula and Real bodies."

"If you ask, so be it. How long did it take?"

"I did not stay up all night . . . There was little time, so I worked as fast as I could, made fast decisions. Luckily, they seemed to work well enough—beginner's luck."

Cormen poked at her delicate ribs. "Apparently making up your mind quickly is part of your nature: you made up your mind fast enough about me."

"Not so!" she said indignantly. There was no decision to make. I mean, I just made straight for you, and I caught you, too . . . Was I too early or too late?" At the last, her playfulness faded into a seemingly genuine sadness, a regret. She did not seem to want an answer to her question, nor did she give any hint to Cormen to understand her meaning.

She returned to her Productions. "I also made up some metamusic: *The Day on Fire,* an adaptation of James Ramsey Ullman's biography of Arthur Rimbaud, done as a triple set by Blue Oyster Cult. Also a Bartok cycle based on a deceptively simple piece he composed called 'Two Portraits'; but here, instead of one girl seen two ways, are five girls seen in different circumstances. I found them rather at random in the Views. It's called 'Working Girls.' "

Cormen looked up at the ceiling. "Bartok's damn difficult, so I understand."

"I found a good splice-on by luck, so it seems."

"By the same fortune, you might instead have happened onto *The Miraculous Mandarin,* or some other of his impossible works. This happened to an old friend once, and it so distressed him he couldn't work on his productions for weeks."

"Well, 'Working Girls' isn't difficult. It's rather simple, easy, although it's subtle, too, but it really is very pleasant, very relaxing. And if you listen very closely, you can almost get a fuzzy image in your mind of the girls, and that disturbs me, because I don't know how it could be. It's just music."

Cormen said, "Richard Strauss was held to believe that he could compose music in which the listener could tell the color of hair of the actress who might play such a heroine."

Faero clapped her hands, like a child. "Say, now. When was this Strauss?"

"Early century twenty."

"Oh, wonderful! Then they were at this before we had MEC to do it for us!"

"Deghil says that a machine is in reality only a standardized method of doing what everybody wants to do; first people do something, in a lot of different ways, with some overlap between them, and gradually the overlaps merge, and when they converge, then you can make a machine to do the job—whatever it is."

"Just like that?"

"Yes."

"What about the knowledge? How do they know how?"

"They cut and fit and use what they have to, and they think up all sorts of tricks to get around the things they can't do—but do anyway, and the knowledge is just a by-product of the desired activity, which in turn is nothing but the expression of dreams and desires, some not very well formed, most poorly integrated and controlled."

"You understand this view?"

"Somewhat . . . It makes some sense."

"Then what happens when people achieve what they really want?"

"Then they do that thing to the exclusion of all else, if they are able."

"That is more disturbing than your worry about the size of the city, or where it really is in relation to the Views. I could become frightened by that, I think."

"No need of that."

"And after learning this, you are giving up your project?"

"Yes, in essense. We have, more or less, what we want. What I want, I suppose. Yes. And you complete it—and perhaps there is something to this—to have a lover in person."

Faero reflected a moment, then said, "There are differences: I will be here in the morning, and we will have to make adjustments and allowances for each other. Nobody's done that in a long time, so no one knows how anymore. And your project—you could turn away from it, just like that?"

Cormen was puzzled by her insistence. "Yes. No hedging. This event with Deghil came when it was needed, a propitious time, as it were. You see, Faero, here in the city-now, we have no evil, no bad mischances, no malevolent wills, such as we can all see in the Views. *There*, they were all unhappy most of the time. *They* had fear, apprehension, worry, dissatisfaction, resentment, hate, Envy. They distrusted nature, they distrusted civilization, they distrusted each other, they distrusted everything. Well, *we* all have our little private vices, which we assiduously cultivate like herbs in a windowsill pot; but *we* commit no heinous crimes, no oppressions, no violences. In a sense, we live in paradise. Why, then, should we worry where or when it is?''

He continued, "Then, I felt we were missing something vital about the nature of our world. I mean, consider the fact that there are no walls, fences, barriers, nothing hinders us from just walking away from it. Nothing. But how would we live? There is no food out there, save the wild things. We could order weapons from MEC, but who knows how to use them, and what happens when they break, out there? To leave, one would have to give everything up, start over from scratch. The gap is too great for us to bridge, *and we all know it*. And so I came to think that we were here for a very good reason, and that if I went too far, I would in the end perceive something I really didn't want to know—perhaps awaken some evil.''

Faero finished the unspoken thought, in many ways an unspeakable one: "You aver that we are all innocent, and that one can only lose that once, and afterward comes tarnish. And there, we cannot pretend.''

He looked off, and mused, "Once, I went east, into the dunes, one whole day's walk from the city. The emptiness frightened me. I looked in vain for signs of others—even our keepers, if that were the case. Lights in the sky, footprints, scraps of machines, discarded things. There was nothing but the wind and the sounding sea and the crying of the sea birds and the strange voices of the animals. The silence said,

'Do you really want to *know?* Part of the answer can't be given. All or nothing.' . . . I was very hungry when I came back, and after that, I explored a few more ruins, then none at all. From time to time, I worked on it. And then this thing with Deghil happened, and you, who are the best and sweetest of all. And so I chose." Cormen here put his hand on the girl's bare, sand-colored thigh, a gesture of affection as well as desire. He said, "This, whatever it is, dream or lost colony or limbo. The taste of your skin."

Faero looked away, sharply, and Cormen thought that somehow he had offended her. "What's wrong?"

She said, slowly, "Cormen, that was the real work of your life; no one else knew, although some wondered at your strange ideas and words. And Nilufer— she knew, but she was amazed by it, dazzled . . ."

He shook his head. "No. I'll not go back to it. I saw that I did not really want the Whole Answer . . ."

". . . Who would?"

". . . And so I have all my indeces, and Productions, and now, the highest of all circles to show them in; and in you a wild talent to urge me to more excellence."

"Oh, I fear that we might become rivals: this must not be."

"We can inspire without envy—the keys are open to all."

Faero looked at him intently. "Some use them well, and others do not, and so are lost forever."

"True! But those things do not apply to you: I see that. So you must come into the world. But now, come with me and we will sleep." He yawned, and stretched.

Faero exclaimed, with mock-horror, "Two to a bed?"

"That, and worse. I will stay as long as you would have it."

She said, almost under her breath, "If I had only known, then I could have come sooner . . ."

Cormen did not hear what she said, clearly, and he asked, "What?"

"Nothing. I love you, is all." She placed a last wild grape in his mouth, then gathered her legs under her and stood, while the dim light of the room played along the lines of her bare limbs.

Cormen looked at Faero in wonder, and said, "If I had just one more wish. . . ."

She bent and placed her finger over his mouth. "Do not say it. We are both past bedtime. Haste, there is not. We always have tomorrow."

Together, sleepy, moving like zombies, they turned off everything and went to the bedroom, where they lay down together, and fell asleep almost immediately. And only once during the night did Cormen wake up: it seemed to be because Faero had been having a bad dream. She was moving restlessly, her skin feverish, hot and damp to the touch. Her mouth moved, but no coherent words came. She seemed terribly agitated, in fear and in anger simultaneously. She also displayed strong expressions of emotions Cormen could not identify. At last, she stammered, ". . . No! No! I won't, not now, no! The time for that has passed!" After that outburst, she abruptly became quiet, rolled over on her side toward him, and relaxed; her skin cooled, and her breathing became quiet and regular. He thought it odd, but gave no more thought to it. Everyone occasionally had nightmares. And so he went back to sleep, next to Faero, in the silences of the night.

In the morning, Faero was gone when Cormen woke up. At first, this was so ordinary and everyday that he noticed nothing amiss. But he realized where he was and then it felt exquisitely abnormal. The place next to him where she had slept was cool. Cormen became concerned, agitated, worried, and went all about the house until he found a small note taped to the door, in her own handwriting, presumably, which explained that she had been called unexpectedly back to work, and expected to be gone most of the morning. He examined the note closely. Cormen was no graphologist, but the writing, at once sprawling and erratic, did not seem to match well with the delicate and precise girl he knew. *Or,* he thought, *thought I knew. Maybe this was why people turned to Simulas. Primes had too many loose ends. One became entangled in them.*

He ordered breakfast and, after eating, decided to straighten things up a little before he left. He was also enjoying the very odd emotional experience of being in another's house, and he wished to savor it a little longer before he left. There was also, still that disturbing hint of déjà-vu, which he still seemed unable to place. He hoped to catch a stronger hint by looking about some.

Cormen imagined that he would find objects of art, pictures, statuary, which reflected their owner, an expanded image. Faero was indeed lovely, and so he anticipated finding more works by Rosamond, or perhaps photographs by David Hamilton. Those also had been on the list he had given her. Of these, he found none. The bedroom was in part a workroom, which he could now see in the daylight. There were pictures and paintings on the walls, but they surprised him. One large canvas, an oil, took up most of one wall; it was a metapainting, by Rembrandt Van Rijn—projected far into Rembrandt's future, called, according to the title plate, "Richard Nixon and his Closest Advisors Hear a Disturbing Report by G. Gordon Liddy." In the painting, the atmosphere was one of intense emotion, in dim lighting, and to a man, the faces glowered with thoughts Cormen could only guess at. Although the metapainting was indeed indistinguishable from a real Rembrandt (in truth, it *was* a Rembrandt), it had a subtle air of having been made, not from imagination, but from reality itself. Cormen knew none of the characters, but something about them suggested that Faero had first photographed a part of the Views, and then run the result through the painting program. Maybe even taped that meeting. It had that subtle air of recorded reality that he knew well.

On the other wall, opposite, toward the rest of the house, was displayed a group of prints, presumably photographs, superbly caught at the precise moment, of a costumed figure grasping a microphone under intense, garish lighting which lent a ghastly quality,

unreal, to the performer. Cormen recognized the figure from his own work with the group Genesis—it
was Peter Gabriel. In one print, he wore an enigmatic
angular prism of a headdress, or mask, and leered
madly at the audience from eyes circled in fluorescent paint. In another, he wore a Nehru jacket and
was made up in blackface. In yet another, he played
a flute, but wore a headband that supported a pair of
gauze batwings behind his head. Another showed
him suspended in a wire harness above the stage,
exhorting the audience to incredible emotions. Why
Gabriel?

In the rest of the house, he found a series of
exquisitely detailed surrealistic drawings, paintings
of multi-armed wizards, beckoning shamans, giant
birds in riding harnesses, machines that looked like
insects, or insects that looked like machines. These
were works by Roger Dean, according to the plates,
and most of them were, apparently, Originals. Again,
as with the handwriting, he felt a discontinuity, a
variation. A curious person, this Faero.

In a secluded corner, he came upon a stack of
discarded prints, neatly set out of the way for later
disposal, obviously property of the former tenant.
Cormen looked through these as well: these were
commonplace and vulgar—waif children with enormous eyes and young animals in the same style,
attributed to a Keane. There were also some scenes
of glittering ballrooms and nightclubs by a Leroy
Neiman, and groups of urchins by a Ted DeGrazia.
Cormen shook his head; he agreed with Faero: they
must go. But oddly, the feeling of déjà-vu was strong-

est about these pictures. Very strong. He had seen them before. But where, and in what context?

He shrugged, giving up for the moment, and left the house, walking back to his own neighborhood by way of a detour along the beach for some distance. It was a fine morning, with crystalline air, and the breeze off the sea was cool and refreshing. Along the way, he reviewed the list of works he had in mind to select from to take to the sobrana at Sofiya Sobranamest tomorrow night.

He spent the rest of the day reviewing possible combinations, collecting and pursuing references, checking examples and trials, using the compositional program of MEC. And toward the end of the afternoon, while he was resting, when the time of day was sifting imperceptibly from afternoon into evening, but was not either, Faero came, tired and silent, but with soft expressions of affection and emotion which soon ripened into passion and desire, and he found it all reassuring and complete. They spent the rest of the evening and the night alternating compositional work with sessions of what Faero called, charmingly, "Flowery Combat." It was, in short, a most entertaining and exhausting evening.

Cormen was surprised and pleased to find that her ardor and her loving-kindness had increased, if anything. But he did note that at times, she seemed distracted and preoccupied; more than once he would look up from his work as they sat on the floor, and see her lips moving slightly, soundlessly, as if she were talking to herself, a frown of concentration obscuring the clear and lovely lines of her face. Very late, she excused herself, promising to return and meet him at his house in time for them to go together to the sobrana. Equally binding, she promised to return again after a few days' rest for them alone, arrayed as he might wish. Cormen, having enjoyed Faero's slight, supple body to the utmost, sighed deeply, smiling weakly, and groaned. But he knew he would recover, and said, "Come to me in the moonlight, radiant in pearls and vetiver and hair-fine chains of gold and electrum. We will taste the rarest vintages to the dregs. Saluté."

She stood by the doorway for a moment, looking pensive and perfectly innocent, although slightly rumpled, and mused, "Pearls and vetiver and gold? The scent, vetiver, I will wear, for I love its grassy pungent sweetness, but the rest must be opals and platinum. Otherwise, it will be as you say . . ." And with the faintest of smiles, she turned and left, walking back to her little house, often stopping to look back, fondly.

The next day, Cormen prepared his productions and rested. The day outside was a good one to avoid-with-work, for it was brazen and sultry, sometimes almost clouding over. There was no breeze at all. The sun sank slowly into a glassy sea the color of wet slate, floating and shimmering. Even far above the horizon, it had been colored a dull orange. And in the still dusk, Faero came, dressed in a soft blue wraparound with large, loose sleeves, wearing enormous blue flowers in her hair. She looked rare and delicate, something tropical from an unknown jungle

world far away. For the moment, all of her earlier
moodinesses had vanished entirely, and again she
was as gay and innocent as a child, ever so slightly
wanton and adventurous.

They arrived fashionably late: a number of people
were already present. To the sides, tables were laid
with delectables of every sort. Deghil and his friends
certainly did not stint on the provender, mere nutriment thought it might be. Cormen, however, noticed
something about the group almost at once which
excited the curiosity he had sworn to suppress. It
seemed that there were two groups present, two very
distinct types. Deghil and his associates proper could
easily be distinguished by their subtlety and restraint,
and an air of elegant measure in all things. Indeed, in
some ways, they were hardly visible. The others,
which were somewhat fewer, were very noticeable
and in most cases rather bizarre. But they seemed to
behave themselves well enough. It surprised him
greatly. Aside from the worst of Embara Park, he
had hardly known such types existed in such numbers,
or that they would come to a sobrana hosted by the
redoubtable Deghil.

They were met by Deghil himself, accompanied by
a girl-child of striking and original appearance: she
was child-slender, almost to the point of starvation,
and her skin had a pale complexion that seemed
never to have been illuminated by any light other
than fluorescent lighting. A pallor. She wore a limp
leather jumpsuit, very thin, whose access was by
means of a large and obvious neck-to-crotch zipper
attached to a parachutist's D-ring. It was now pulled

open to her navel. On her thin neck she wore a choker of black fabric, ornamented with silver and turquoises. The girl managed to appear perverse, wanton, and as perilous as forbidden drugs and forgotten rites, all at once. Deghil introduced her as one Roxanne Doymaz. The girl mumbled a few ill-said false pleasantries, and then excused herself to do some serious nibbling. Faero declared herself hungry as well, and joined the girl by one of the tables.

Cormen would have gone with them, but Deghil held back, as if there were more that he wished to say. Cormen said, after some hesitation, "I would not be rude, but I do find it curious that a person of your reputation would come to a sobrana such as this with a girl like Roxanne. Am I missing something I should know, or must I feel my way along?"

Deghil smiled and said, "Well, you might have noticed that many of us are accompanied by certain persons of perhaps dubious character."

"Indeed! Thugs, purveyors of vice, girls of the worst sort of nighted wickedness." Something suggested that he should be bold, and so he spoke frankly.

Deghil said, engimatically, "These, ah, escorts do not seem to be part of the circle . . ."

"No. But I still don't understand."

"But you must! It couldn't be otherwise!"

"No. I am serious."

"You stroke me!"

"I swear, not a word!"

Deghil said, thoughtfully, "Perhaps, perhaps . . . Very well, I will risk face, then. The ones who are

different . . . they are all simulas. We bring them out
on certain occasions, as it were, for purposes of
mutual exhibition. We all have, of course, many to
draw on, but it never hurts to repeat one's successes,
does it? My Roxanne, for example, is a most perverse half-child, half-woman, and half something utterly unspeakable!" He chuckled. "We go searching
for them in Time, in the Views. And that, of course,
was one of our reasons for bringing you in—at Brasille,
you were seen with that delightful, marvelous creature,
and all agreed that she had to be a Simula, and that
your taste was virtually perfect. And now you can't
mean to tell me that this Faero Sheftali is a Prime! I
would never have known!"

Cormen stuttered. "As far as I know, she's Prime,
just as you and I."

"Curious, curious. There is simply no end to the
marvels that MEC can reproduce through the House of
Life, is there? Its creations are sometimes more . . .
vivid than ours, however hard we try. And so then I
ponder, I wonder, I consider: impossible, but perhaps
it is Faero who is Prime, and Cormen who is the
Simula."

Cormen hid the irritation he felt and said, "Not so,
Ser Deghil: I have a Call-Code." Struck with
inspiration, he added, "You may claim it of me, if
you desire."

Deghil was unperturbed, and replied, "Excellent.
A most excellent fellow, fit to join us indeed. And so
we may speak of this later. But for now, I must greet
more latecomers, so please excuse me."

Cormen, left alone, looked to the buffet, and there

saw Roxanne and Faero, sampling things and talking animatedly, as if they had become fast friends, or already knew one another. Cormen joined the two girls, sampling the tidbits with them, and trying to remain tactful and discreet in the face of what Deghil had told him. Simulas at home was one thing, but out in the open, like this, in public? It was madness; although not terribly different, when he reflected on it.

He noticed that Roxanne appraised him openly, not bothering to conceal her interest in him from Faero, who in turn gave no sign that she was interested in that at all. Cormen looked closely at the pale, skinny form of the girl, and caught himself thinking that perhaps in some circumstances, Roxanne could be an intriguing diversion. She had a bratty, worldly-wise face with childish features, thin, colorless lips. But strange! He saw that she had chewed her fingernails to nubs, so at the least, she wouldn't scratch. . . . And he wondered how Deghil had found her: in the Views, he had said, somewhere in Time. Yes. She bore the aspect of someone from Time.

A disturbing vision caught at his flow of thoughts, a late response to Deghil's cynical banter: who, indeed, were Simulas, and who were Prime? Cormen had always selected his Simulas from those he saw around him, in the streets, at sobrany, in the parks. They were, in their originals, like him, no more, no less. But there was something about those from Time; they seemed . . . what? More clearly defined, perhaps, better-focused. He felt his perceptual world shift a

little, a tiny bit, after the way of a nightmare or an
earthquake, and during this, he also saw that Faero
shared that vivid sense of sharpness, the same quality
that made her so real and desirable. He shook his
head, as if to clear the unreal vision away, and the
old perception returned, trembling and somewhat tentative now. And then he was caught up in the swirls
and currents of Deghil's sobrana.

Much later, when the ranks of partygoers had begun
to thin out, and the earnest conversations had slowed
to tangents and hazy, blurred repetitions, slightly
drunk, Cormen excused himself from a conversation
with a group of some of Deghil's close friends, and
went looking for Faero, who was now unaccountably
gone. She had been just behind him but a moment
ago. Now he looked carefully, but he did not find her
among the remaining guests. He searched the rest of
the grounds of the Sobranamest: the Buffet, the kitchen
beyond, all around the outer perimeter. Discreetly,
he knocked on the bathroom doors; she was in none
of those places.

Somewhat confused, disoriented and dulled by the
champagne he had consumed—Modesto Brut 81,
Cormen tried to recall something, something important,
but nothing came. He could not recall any arrangements. But dimly, he did recall something about
Faero saying that she was feeling bad . . . over-
extended, she had said. Yes, that. Perhaps she had
gone home. And in any event, she would be in no
shape for further adventures. After making the proper
motions and excuses, Cormen left Sofiya, and started

walking home. As he left, he observed, half smiling to himself, that a hardy few of the free-adventurers were still prowling among the worn plantings and shrubberies of Embara Park, still profiling, still posturing, trying their best.

But along the long way home, his head cleared somewhat, so that by the time he reached his own neighborhood, he was more or less himself, if a little tired. And he caught himself thinking, *the circle of Deghil—was that such an honor, then?* All he had heard from those he had met this night were references to works of strange and disturbing outline, dissonant musics which produced hallucinatory states of mind and heart, exquisitely morbid styles and modes borrowed from obscure artists best forgotten. Or else, of Viewpoints in Time of questionable spectacles, tragedies, disasters. *And these were the ultimate pinnacles?* Did one have to choose between— and only—Keane waifs, and The Last Days of Pompeii, Live in color from 79 AD? Cormen felt that his ambition had been shattered beyond repair. Had Faero suspected this was coming?

As he entered his own house, he found himself missing the odd, unique girl greatly. For a long time after he turned on the lights, he walked around the house aimlessly, thinking, trying to decide, or avoid a decision. At last, with a resigned sigh, he sat on the floor by the MEC mainframe, and, opening a small cabinet, removed a helmet-like device of complicated, asymmetrical shape, connected to the console through a heavy, twisted umbilical, and put it on his head. Under the headset, Cormen summoned every image of Faero he could recall: Thoughtful. Gayly abandoned, her pretty face flushed with innocent lust and passion, with that odd, pensive smile, slow and lazy, of a woman joined with her chosen lover. In truth, Cormen never used the headset much, and he found the side-effects it induced to be most unpleasant: one's limbs felt distorted, the eyeballs felt furry. His scalp crawled, and strange half-visions crawled across the eye of his memory, some merely obscene, others nightmarishly distorted. And he knew a Truth, that the hardest feat of memory was remembering the face of one you loved deeply. Never casual, it was an act of the hardest concentration.

And as yet, nothing had happened: it was taking far too long! He reached and felt by his right ear, and depressed the interrogate button, sharply, as if to say, "Well? Get on with it!"

A ringing sound told him that the scan was finished: Cormen removed the headset, feeling drugged and dumb. With heavy eyes, he looked at the readout screen on the console, as letters swam into view as if floating up from the bottom of a pool of ink, flowing together to form words, like some abstract ballet. The words said:

IMAGE INVALID

Cormen thumbed the interrogate button again. The screen trembled, faded the flowing, loose seaweed words, and formed more, with that greasy certitude. It replied:

IMAGE IS INVALID. NO RECORD OF
SUCH ENTITY IN REFERENCE STORAGE

STOP NO CODE STOP REQUEST VERIFICA-
TION STOP HEADSET NOW RESET MARK

Cormen watched the letters fade, and then softly
spoke a very obscene word in a language long
forgotten. This was an impossible situation: if you
were a person, walking about, you had to exist.
Existing, your Call-Code could be found, and a Simula
could be printed on you. It was at this exact moment
that Cormen, his mind overstimulated by the headset,
remembered that Faero had asked him to promise that
he would not try to find her Call-Code and order a
Simula. And she did not give her Call-Code out. But
she had to exist: he knew this. He could remember
vividly how the afternoon sunlight had fallen on their
bodies through the window, on her brown legs with
their faint aureola of fine golden hair, for she did not
depilate her body, anywhere. Indeed, Faero was the
most real of any person he had known in the memory
of his life in the city. And without a Call-Code, he
couldn't even call her. How could he find her code?
He felt a sudden need to speak to her, to be near her,
to go to her, immediately. He could go directly, but a
curious feeling moved him in this: that as intimate as
they had been, he also sensed a fastidious privateness
about her person, and he hesitated to go without
calling her in some way. But how? And it also came
to him, out of nowhere, where he had seen those
pictures before, the ones in the stack on the floor in
Faero's house. They had been Nilufer's! Faero lived
in Nilufer's house. And Nilufer was gone, after he
and Faero had met. Coincidence? Cormen struggled

now with concepts he had only known in the Views and in the Arts—suspicion, concealed motivation, secrets, evasions, omissions: Alien Thoughts. These did not exist in City-Now. Only *there*, in the bowels of wicked Time. In Art, which was a product of Time.

He got up unsteadily and went to the communicator, where he dialed in Nilufer's number and followed it with an imperative command code, that the number of that house be called no matter what. After a moment, the screen started to clear, but it flickered and distorted badly, unable to form a coherent image. But he did catch momentary glimpses of the house, as if the Pickup circuits were cycling erratically. Yes! There! The Peter Gabriel prints, and then a quick shot of Faero, face blurred, on her knees by the bed, trying to look at him, speaking, moving her lips, but no sound came: only the faint buzz of static. And then the screen went blank, and abruptly became a mirror once again. Then shattered into pellets. Now it was just a frame, with some colored wiring and enigmatic devices behind it.

Cormen turned from the communicator and left the house, pausing only to pick up his night-cape from the coat-closet where he had left it.

There was a heaviness to the night left over from the day, a tiredness to the air that the sea winds of evening had failed to clear away: a sullen quality. Along the way to her house, Nilufer's, Faero's, Cormen felt an odd emotion, composed of fear, of dread, of foreboding, and of the piquant sense of the forbidden: *One does not go to another's house*. But

he had, and now he was going again, likely into
something unpleasant, a thing they of the City did
not face. He had no idea at all what he might do; or
what he might find at the house of Faero, the house
of Nilufer.

This went through his head: *All the suffering, all
the worry, all the passions and extravagant acts—
those were the legacy of the Views, which the Arts
were connected with somehow, because they dealt
with the same things, but with altered weights and
different priorities. But now that part of the Views
was intruding into the City, which had been immune.
Had he and Faero somehow broken some unspoken com-
mandment by what they had done? It had seemed
such a small matter, just different.* But now he hurried on to her house.

At the house, all the lights were on, while the other
houses were dark: their tenants were asleep or else
the houses were empty. Many were in this quarter,
near the sea. This would be the next section abandoned.
Cormen hurried up to the door, past the fragrant
shrubs, and saw that it was standing open, and the
bright light inside was pouring out into the night.
Wrong, wrong. He stopped, hesitated—and then went
in.

In the living room, nothing. There were some
things out of place, but no indication of anyone: he
crossed the open space, feeling watched, open,
vulnerable. In the hall, the pile of old pictures was
still just as he had left them: Faero had not yet
thrown them out. There was no one in the bedroom,

either. The bed was rumpled in total disorder. The
bath was empty. Cormen started back, confused and
unfocused: *something* he had anticipated. An empty
house left him at loose ends, unaimed, unmotivated.
As he rounded the corner of the bath, he saw an untidy
scrawl on the wall which he had missed earlier,
because of the angle. It was only chance that he saw
it. In was in pale lipstick, and was only one word:
TAPE. It was barely legible. Tape?

He looked about, uncertain. There was no tape to
be seen among the disarray of the bedroom. He
returned to the living room and searched. By the
mainframe, there was a reel of tape, next to the
composition section. Normally, a work-in-progress
would be stored in MEC, so there was little need for
taped records; but sometimes people used tapes to
record references, when doing rapid-scans through a
time or over an area-cover. Things to come back to,
sometime. This appeared to be such a tape. It would
play back through an ordinary reproducer without
going back through MEC central. When he bent to
pick it up, he saw a faint mark on the reel, a streak of
the same kind of pale lipstick. He wiped the mark
off, and inserted the reel in the reproducer.

The voice began shortly; it was her voice, no
doubt, but distorted, as if she were having trouble
breathing. The voice said, ". . . I left this to explain,
as much as I can. I have to go back to the House of
Life. I thought I could resist, but now I know that
this is impossible. I know I am going. Only this."

There was a long pause, in which he could only
hear her rasping, struggling breathing. Then, ". . .

You must have tried by now to call, and you couldn't, because I never had a call-code. And if you tried the headset, you will have found that you can't get a Simula of me, because I don't exist. But I do exist. This is true. So it was . . . We all come from the House of Life, all alike, Prime and Simula. There is no difference. MEC populates the City according to the averaging trends it senses in the requests, and so as the trends change, so do the newcomers it creates and trains and releases. The images are drawn from the Views, records MEC has of real people who lived in Time, in the Views. You and I, we have been before, perhaps many times. This is entropic, so MEC inserts at random intervals, odd sorts into the roster of Primes, to stir things up. Most of these are unsuccessful and quickly fail, and return early, after causing a little change. You were one of the rare odd ones who did not fail . . . but was succeeding, and more—you were on the edge of seeing into the true nature of things. MEC could extrapolate from your requests for data, even while it was making it harder and harder for you; but it had not faced such a situation before. It can only judge us according to the Game rules in it. Once released, it cannot exercise arbiter authority.

"There is only one difference between Primes and Simulas: the Prime Persona endures according to the rules of the Credit Section, and is essentially uncontrolled, although its actions are registered and filed. Simulas are controlled by various means, but they themselves are not aware of such control. . . . But the emerging pattern of your actions set off alarms which hadn't rung in—time uncounted and unknown. Most of the alarms were inoperable from age. The instructions were unclear, possibly from an overlay of daily actions which had blurred the Instructions of the Original Makers of MEC. So it made me up to judge you, Cormen. It took one of its patterns and brought me to Life, only to pass judgement on you, for only a Prime can ultimately judge another Prime, beyond MEC's sphere of competence. This I did according to my instructions . . . and it rescinded my judgment, and went the other way. I loved you and for this I was rated a flawed unit, one that had failed. And so I am called back. You are safe, now, for the while . . . but it will send another like me, sometime, to read you again, maybe many of them, one after another until one will pass judgment on you the way it wishes it done. Maybe another me, maybe someone else. I do not know that. I know that it knows the things you like best.''

The voice on the tape now stopped, but Cormen could still hear breathing, labored and difficult. At last, the voice said, ''I wanted very much to stay, but it has become too much to resist any longer; I cannot. I have to go back to the House of Life. But I wanted, I hoped to draw you to my house to find this, that you would know . . . and because Nilufer was so much your true friend, I would also tell you that she went to make room for me, for the City population can only be so many, and the exemption overload period had expired. I was both Prime and Simula, and it held me in the City longer because of what I was to have done . . .'' It trailed off, again, and

Cormen thought that this might be all. But she coughed, and spoke again, now very weakly. "I wish I could stay to tell you everything, that I could stay and spend an entire life with you, but I have held out against Summons for a whole day . . . I thought perhaps I could beat it, that it might leave me alone . . . not to be so. The TimeSpace coordinates for my Original Imago are written in my work-log above the main-frame . . . please call for her—she is me, even though she will not remember the sweet things we did . . . do some more with her . . . I . . . It's now. Good-bye." The tape ended.

He looked, dumbly, in the place she had indicated, and found a hastily written set of TimeSpace coordinates, azimuth and range. The range was very short, about two meters, which indicated that the Original in Time was inside a building, or else in a crowd. He would have to actually set it to see. He put the piece of paper in his pocket, absentmindedly, shaking his head, numbly. *So that was how she had caught on so fast!* She had come into the world with more knowledge about the way they did things than he could have ever manged to assemble in his workbooks. And Deghil suspected, sure enough, and also Roxanne—perhaps they shared some kind of Simula-empathy. Perhaps. All that, and he still felt a vast bottomless ache in his heart. Not that he had been spied on, but that he had lost something priceless, forever. Not her body, but her heart. Cormen got up abruptly and ran out of the house, turning for the center of the City as fast as he could go. He thought that there still might be some time, and that if he could be there, then somehow his being there might make some difference, might help her remain free. A sober part of him told him in a cold, echoing voice that it would make no difference, that MEC would take her back, because it had given her too much of a headstart; under the universal credit rules. Faero as she was would always prosper—she had too much to start with. No wonder she hadn't gravitated toward Embara Park.

The House of Life was a plain stone building set near the center of the City, severely plain, a simple cubical structure without windows. A tall, narrow door under a plain portico seemed to be the only lines added to its plainness. Most of the time, the people avoided this location: one could always go in, voluntarily, if circumstances were such. But no one ever came back. That was the way it was: you could emerge only once.

He approached it from its back side, the steps, door, and portico invisible. At a half-trot, breathless, he rounded the corner, and in the uncertain light, thought he saw a dim figure walking up the steps. He called out, "Faero, Faero, wait!"

The dim figure hesitated, looked about, but went on up the steps. Cormen ran now, with the last reserves of his strength, gasping for air. All around him, the night was still and silent, mocking his exertion, his passions. He reached the steps and looked up, and saw a slight, trim girl standing in the half-open door, lit from behind with a soft, golden light, silhouetting her form through the thin material of her clothing. She paused, and looked back, across the City, the plaza of the House of Life, and last, at him, with a wistful, infinitely sad look to what he could see of her face. She turned away, abruptly, and went inside, and the door closed silently after her, and Cormen Demir-Hisar stood at the foot of the steps, one foot on the first step, staring at the blank face of an unmarked door which would not open, unless he himself opened it. He was breathing hard, and one thought stood within his mind like a Monolith: *We did not even have a chance to say good-bye.*

The night was late, silent, and the city was empty; its emptiness hung over the City like fog in the still-heavy air. For a long time, Cormen stood at the foot of the steps going up to the House of Life, not thinking, hardly breathing, unable to act. Shreds and shards of past Productions echoed in his mind, mixed in impossible conjunctions, threaded along a tangled string of his own thoughts, now fragmentary and broken: Now. Henry Cowell's Eleventh Symphony. An opera, *The Transposed Heads,* by Peggy Glanville-Hicks, directed by the redoubtable Moritz Bomhard. Boris Blacher's *Studie im Pianissimo.* Carl Orff's *Carmina Burana,* complete with Disney animation after the manner of *Fantasia,* with retranslation by Aleister Crowley (here, a note: Dropped—much too demonic, especially the finale "*Fortuna Imperatrix Mundi,*" C. D-H). And then *When the door to the House of Life has closed, all the questions are answered, but the answer cannot be sent back. I could now go there, where she has gone, but it is the Silence and the Nothingness.* Then, *Gulag,* a metamusic opera, projected-by Modest Mussorgsky, based on Solzhenitsyn; George London, tenor. Performed by Leopola Stokowski (Also rearranged by the old master) and the Louisville Symphony, an orchestra long noted for performing difficult and taxing experimental works. (Here, another mental note: Much too long—after ten hours the audience tends to catatonia and/or delerium. C. D-H.) And then, *Alternately, of what use to return to the old world and act as if nothing untoward has happened? It was for us the best of all conditions, that we became, for a moment, that which we now see only in the Views—Reality. There is a pain to this that cannot be treated, ignored, or entertained away. An emptiness. If this is the artifact of Love, I do not wonder that we—whoever we are—chose the simple gratifications of Simulas. Eros can be anagrammed into Rose. Also Sore.* (Here, a research note: Even pressed hard by MEC, Mussorgsky remains intractable, producing two or three immense, impossible operas in bunches which tend to occur every fifty or sixty years, usually on some cataclysmic subject from history, for example, *The Warsaw Ghetto, Dien Bien Phu, Hiroshima, Jonestown, Entebbe.* Etc. Hopeless. Mussorgsky, even projected beyond his own Original TimeSpace lifespan by MEC, even in metamusic, never learns that to create is to know when to stop!). *Aha. When to stop. I have stopped. Pepauka. Something in me has ended. This is—has been—nonsense, from the Beginning. What was real was us and what we gave freely. I was learning.* Wagner's *Rise and Fall of Adolf Hitler*, with libretto adapted from the diaries of Dr. Goebbels, filmed live at Reichswahn, an open-air theater on the classical Greek model of amphitheater, given over to musical legends in alternate history of the raging demons of National Socialism. (Note: Must refer to Direct Views of referenced period. This material is so fantastic that it almost has to be based on some fantasy work of the period by a deranged maniac. C. D-H.) Orson Welles playing the Baron Vladimir Harkonnen; Arnold Schwartzenegger as Conan. David Jansen as Gilbert Gosseyn. James Caan as Gully Foyle. Stop. STOP.

Cormen slowly turned away, a movmeent that felt centuries long, never-ending; and began to walk away from the plaza of the House of Life. He did not know where he was going, only that he was going, wherever his steps took him. The clamor in his mind died away, leaving a silence as empty as the city behind it. Cormen walked on.

A soft, pearlescent glow was streaking the lower skirts of the sky, but the stars were still shining overhead, Orion ascendant, when Cormen stopped and sat on a crumbling wall, and looked back south over the city. He felt like Lot's wife, but he did not turn to salt. The City flowed softly as carpet down to the gentle sea, the tropical waters of the bay. He could sense his favorite View emerging from the darkness—the distant palms of the Bay Islands—mere sandbars far out over the water.

Beauty? Beauty was something internally secret

and unknown which translated into exteriors; now he knew it. A state of the inner persona, a balance, an orientation. Desire they had known, but within it there had been moments of Something Else for which they now had no word or name. They shared, how-ever small that sharing had been. They had reached together for the forbidden apples of Derketo, and learned why they were forbidden. And she, Faero, the spy in the house of love, had tried to become free of the dream even though she knew well the price. She knew, from the beginning.

He stood up and stretched; he saw the day spread-ing in light, the stars fading, the City and MEC waiting for him to return and complete the cycle of what had been started. He felt a wry face forming, something between a grimace and a snarl, a tic that lasted only a moment. Yes—he would complete something. He would splice onto the old track, the old curiosity line, and take it up, here, now. *Let the old wait forever. I can walk away from it, and there has to be a place from which it can't call me back.* To be sure, he knew regrets for the things that he would not do again: food on request; a lovely girl seen—and enjoyed later at his own leisure. The unde-niable thrill of working up a new Production. In place of these pleasant knowns, he set unknowns: hunger, fear, thirst. Fear: yes, there would be fear. Death. Not re-entering the House of Life. Cormen shrugged, looked around once, twice, and started out into the north, the future, without comment or anticipation. It was the unthinkable choice, but something in him had stirred, and demanded that he at least try. He would never know, otherwise.

But Cormen grew a lot hungrier before he found an answer, and that one did not really answer the question he wanted most to know. It might have been a long day—or perhaps two days which had passed quickly. At times he could not be sure. Leaving the pleasant seacoast lands of the City, he had walked some distance through a scrub-covered hinterland of sandy soil and occasional dense tangles of low trees—or high bushes. After that, the ground began to rise and an open pine forest took over. He found water, but very little to eat. Wild animals avoided him, or remained invisible, or simply weren't. He didn't know. Perhaps it was only their wildness and his strangeness, for he was sure that there was no sign whatsoever of men or their works.

As the night approached, Cormen began to see fugitive gleams of a single point of light through the trees. It did not waver or move, but it seemed weak, ghostly, and far away; at times he lost sight of it completely. But as it became darker, the light through the trees seemed to strengthen, and become easier to follow, and Cormen followed it to whatever might be.

After many detours, including wading and half-running across a sluggish river ripe with the odor of decaying vegetation, Cormen cautiously approached the light, which appeared to be emanating from a translucent fixture of no great size set atop a starkly simple small building. For a time, he remained in the

forest and watched carefully; but here, as through the
rest of the pine forest, there was no sign of men or
indeed any form of moving life. The building was a
cylindrical drum supporting an ogival dome, made of
a rough-textured material that resembled concrete or
some kind of masonry, but which seemed to have
small prisms set within its surface. A shimmer, a
sparkle on the edge of perception. The grounds about
the building were bare, sterile: a sandy zone in which
nothing grew.

He stepped out, onto the open ground, walking
toward the structure, senses alert; behind him, he
thought he heard a low, muffled snort, and some
motion in the brush, *moving away,* and presently
fading completely. As he walked on the bare ground,
he felt a prickling sensation on his skin—exactly like
that of a limb with returning circulation: tiny bright
spots arranged in a hexagonal grid appeared in his
vision. He came closer. The sensations were odd, but
he felt no danger in them.

On the side he had approached from, there was no
door or opening; the drum and the dome appeared to
be cast in one piece. Cautious, Cormen began to
circle around it. It seemed no larger than about ten
meters in diameter. He saw no evidence that anything
approached the building. When he had completed
half a turn around it, he found a simple portal on the
side facing away from the City. There was no latch
or handle. He pushed it experimentally with his hand,
and felt a sharper prickling, although the surface
seemed smooth enough to the eye. Extending his
hand again, now with fingers extended, he pushed at

the door, and it swung open soundlessly, with the least effort.

The inside of the building seemed to be a single chamber, not large, as if the walls were extremely thick. He entered, there was a dry, musty odor, very faint, a sense of stale air long undisturbed. Behind him, the door slid shut. He noticed that there was a plain, serviceable handle on the inside of the door. As for the rest of the interior, it was as bare as the outside, save for a small grille opposite the door, and a shiny plate set into the wall just below it. The light seemed to come from the ceiling, but from the walls, too. He moved closer, and when he got within reach of the wall, he again felt the prickling sensation and the spots in his vision. He looked around. The sourceless light seemed to lend an unreal quality to everything.

The prickling stopped, and the grille emitted a single click. It startled Cormen, the single sound was very loud in the quiet of the chamber. Then, from the grille, a voice spoke. It was clearly the voice of a machine translator, recognizable sounds, slightly blurred and smeared, and utterly without emotional expression or variation of timbre. It said, ''Do you wish to leave the City? If so, depress the plate in the wall, pause, and depart the way you came in. You are authorized. Thank you.''

After a moment, it repeated the message again. And again. Cormen tried to talk back to it, but without result, whatever this machine was, it did not answer. Somehow his entry had activated it, which did not surprise him.

Cormen reached for the plate; and then stopped. He asked himself if he really did want to leave the City. And in that, he weighed many things. Still, he hesitated. This was reality, strange though it was, but like reality, it was also powerfully unknown. Into what would the door lead? He had come through it from the outside. But the machine had said, "Depress the plate, pause, and depart the way you came in." He pressed it, hard, felt a slight electrical shock, and that was all. He withdrew his hand, and said, aloud, "Well, nothing changed. The circuits have long since corroded out of existence. So much for this, whatever it is." He listened carefully. There was no sound, just as before. The air was still stale. Cormen turned away from the wall, downcast. *Betrayed by another machine.* Hungry, tired, thirsty; there was nothing in this building but shelter from the Outside. At least that. He felt safe. But before he rested, he went back to the door, thinking perhaps to prop it open a little, to let some fresh air in.

When he opened the door, he opened it wide and stared, standing for a long time as still as one turned to stone. For outside was no nighted forest, pine or otherwise, but an enclosed landing, covered by some transparent material, and beyond that, an enormous room, or alley, or canyon; he could not tell. To either side were galleries with safety rails, rank upon rank of panels, and people walked those narrow ways, many of them engaged in working along the faces of those panels, which were covered with banks of lights, speakers, switches, knobs, levers, meters, and other devices he couldn't make out. This extended without limit to either side, and up and down as far as he could see, in a dim, obviously artificial light. Directly ahead, the tremendous open space continued indefinitely, although very far off there was a suggestion of something, a barrier, perhaps, or only a series of crossovers. He couldn't see it clearly.

Hesitantly, he stopped into the small chamber. It was almost as bare as the building, but there were some chairs, and a plain metallic table. To either side, a narrow door, out into the open expanses of whatever this was. Cormen sat in one of the chairs, because he couldn't think of anything else to do for the moment.

As he sat, he became conscious of a constant low noise all around him, the hum of energy, of many people, or endless activity, purposeful and powerful. And amid the low noise, he heard footfalls on metal, approaching, not hurrying, but coming at a good pace. In the dimness beyond the enclosure he made out the shapes of a man and a woman, of no immediately distinguishing appearance, save that they were both rather stocky and short, powerful rather than graceful, homely rather than beautiful. Their expressions were curious, as they opened the door, perhaps friendly, in a careful, neutral way.

The woman spoke. "Hello. I am Elit." She indicated the man. "And this is Dant. What is your name?"

"Cormen." Her voice had an odd accent to it, something he couldn't identify. But she spoke confidently enough.

Elit asked, "Have you come from . . . the City?"

"Yes. Where am I? What is this?"

Dant now said, in a lower, gruff voice, "For practical purposes, you may think of this place as a sort of spaceship. It serves as, ah, a kind of communications nexus, a relay station, a switchboard. Yes. Have no fears. You will only be here a short time. Please come with us."

Cormen stood up and made to follow them. Elit said, "There will be a short walk, out there, to your next destination, which will be the world Mola."

Cormen asked, "Who are you?"

She said, "We are Dant and Elit; we are your monitors. There is much that you will need to relearn. Things here are not as they are in the City. Does it really still function?"

"Oh, yes. Perfectly . . . or at least workably, as far as I know."

Elit said, dryly, "It would have to, I imagine. The Chamber admitted you, and it wouldn't have done that unless you were completely human."

"How did you know I was coming?"

Dant said, "We did not know. We were alerted that you had arrived. It was unexpected. There hasn't been anyone for a long time."

They stepped out of the room onto a walkway connecting this section with the far wall. There were rails on the sides of the metallic catwalk, but the drop to either side seemed to have no bottom. Something dim, and far away, hazy. Up, it was much the same. Cormen asked, "You have met others, like me?"

Elit turned back to him. "We? In person? Oh, no. Not in our lifetimes. The last one before you was . . . I think, about three hundred of your years ago, and that one was the first in a long time, too."

Cormen stopped, looked around, frightened. "Which is real?"

Dant said in his gruff voice, but with unmistakable warmth in it, "This is real! That you left was the dream. People made it, long ago; they liked it so much that they couldn't leave it. It wasn't the City: there were many. But some managed to escape, leave, and now we have made a new life out among the stars. You will find it hard at first, I think, but if you left on your own, you will survive here. You can always go back."

"Has anyone ever gone back to the City?"

"Not to my knowledge."

"What is . . . Mola?"

"A planet, a world, a new world we are populating. You will be one of those who builds it. We will teach you what you need to know to begin. First we'll start with language."

"Language?"

"Yes. We speak yours because we learn it just for this task. In fact, you speak a language that has been dead and forgotten for thousands of years. Are you ready, now? Then come with us." And together, the three of them made their way across the catwalk toward the far wall, immense, endless, coming closer, and Cormen followed them, slowly at first, hesitantly, a little reluctantly, but with increasing energy as they neared the far wall, and by the time they had stepped off the catwalk, they were all talking animatedly and sometimes laughing.

*   *   *

There was another sobrana at Brasille, and everyone
was out, as usual dressed in their most impression-
casting clothing. This particular meet was not sponsored by Corymont Deghil and friends, but by a
lesser group; still, the level of manners and taste was
high. One could readily contrast this group with the
amateurs and brash parvenus of Embara Park.

By the serving-table, at a lull in the proceedings,
two young women happened to meet over a selection
of hors d'oeuvres. One was tall and statuesque with
flowing black hair. The other was small and slight,
with skin the color of beach sand, and sharp, crisp
features.

The smaller girl introduced herself as one Faero
Sheftali, and told the other that she was a recent
arrival, but she was learning fast. She had already
met a number of interesting people, and selected
some Productions to review.

The taller woman called herself Nilufer Emeksiz,
and also spoke positively of this particular sobrana.
She added, "I also have a work I will mention to
you, that you may view it at your leisure: *Babel-17,*
By Samuel Delany, done as cinema, animation after
the style of Boris Artsybashieff. Music by Spirogyra.
It's really very interesting. . . ."

Faero removed a small notebook from a conve-
nient pocket in her loose skirt, a pen, and wrote
down the information, as well as a number, which
Nilufer gave her to credit it to. She said, "Thank
you. I will try it . . ." And she gave Nilufer, in
trade, the index numbers of sevreal sculptors of the

twentieth century, and also Giambologna, specifically referring to his work, "The Labors of Hercules." And she said. "You do look familiar. Have we met somewhere?"

Nilufer answered, "I don't think so; but perhaps we saw each other at a distance."

"Yes, that seems likely . . . and by the way, do you have the Call-Code for that young man over there, the light-haired fellow wearing the bush jacket and walking shorts? I haven't been able to get near him all evening."

Nilufer agreed, commenting on Faero's good taste in men, and gave her the number, and after that, they returned to the sobrana. And not long afterward, they separately went back to their own houses to sample some of the things they had uncovered during the evening, and to reflect and be thankful that the world never suffered change, and that these pleasures, innocent enough, might never end.

DAW

DAW BRINGS YOU THESE BESTSELLERS BY
MARION ZIMMER BRADLEY

☐ DARKOVER LANDFALL	UE1906—$2.50
☐ THE SPELL SWORD	UE1891—$2.25
☐ THE HERITAGE OF HASTUR	UE1967—$3.50
☐ THE SHATTERED CHAIN	UE1961—$3.50
☐ THE FORBIDDEN TOWER	UE2029—$3.95
☐ STORMQUEEN!	UE1951—$3.50
☐ TWO TO CONQUER	UE1876—$2.95
☐ SHARRA'S EXILE	UE1988—$3.95
☐ HAWKMISTRESS!	UE1958—$3.50
☐ THENDARA HOUSE	UE1857—$3.50
☐ CITY OF SORCERY	UE1962—$3.50
☐ HUNTERS OF THE RED MOON	UE1968—$2.50
☐ THE SURVIVORS	UE1861—$2.95

Anthologies

☐ THE KEEPER'S PRICE	UE1931—$2.50
☐ SWORD OF CHAOS	UE1722—$2.95
☐ SWORD AND SORCERESS	UE1928—$2.95

DAW

PHILIP K. DICK

"The greatest American novelist of the second half of the 20th Century."

—*Norman Spinrad*

"A genius . . . He writes it the way he sees it and it is the quality, the clarity of his Vision that makes him great."

—*Thomas M. Disch*

"The most consistently brilliant science fiction writer in the world."

—*John Brunner*

PHILIP K. DICK

In print again, in DAW Books' special memorial editions:

☐ **WE CAN BUILD YOU** (#UE1793—$2.50)
☐ **THE THREE STIGMATA OF PALMER ELDRITCH**
(#UE1810—$2.50)
☐ **A MAZE OF DEATH** (#UE1830—$2.50)
☐ **UBIK** (#UE1859—$2.50)
☐ **DEUS IRAE** (#UE1887—$2.95)
☐ **NOW WAIT FOR LAST YEAR** (#UE1654—$2.50)
☐ **FLOW MY TEARS, THE POLICEMAN SAID** (#UE1969—$2.50)
☐ **A SCANNER DARKLY** (#UE1923—$2.50)

DAW

Have you discovered DAW's new rising star?

SHARON GREEN

High adventure on alien worlds with women of talent versus men of barbaric determination!

The Terrilian novels

☐ **THE WARRIOR WITHIN** (#UE1797—$2.50)

☐ **THE WARRIOR ENCHAINED** (#UE1789—$2.95)

☐ **THE WARRIOR REARMED** (#UE1895—$2.95)

Jalav: Amazon Warrior

☐ **THE CRYSTALS OF MIDA** (#UE1735—$2.95)

☐ **AN OATH TO MIDA** (#UE1829—$2.95)

☐ **CHOSEN OF MIDA** (#UE1927—$2.95)

Diana Santee: Spaceways Agent

☐ **MIND GUEST** (#UE1973—$3.50)

DAW

Unforgettable science fiction
by DAW's own stars!

M. A. FOSTER

☐	THE WARRIORS OF DAWN	UE1994—$2.95
☐	THE GAMEPLAYERS OF ZAN	UE1993—$3.95
☐	THE MORPHODITE	UE2017—$2.95
☐	THE DAY OF THE KLESH	UE2016—$2.95

C.J. CHERRYH

☐	40,000 IN GEHENNA	UE1952—$3.50
☐	DOWNBELOW STATION	UE1987—$3.50
☐	VOYAGER IN NIGHT	UE1920—$2.95
☐	WAVE WITHOUT A SHORE	UE1957—$2.50

JOHN BRUNNER

☐	TIMESCOOP	UE1966—$2.50
☐	THE JAGGED ORBIT	UE1917—$2.95

ROBERT TREBOR

☐	AN XT CALLED STANLEY	UE1865—$2.50

JOHN STEAKLEY

☐	ARMOR	UE1979—$3.95

JO CLAYTON

☐	THE SNARES OF IBEX	UE1974—$2.75

DAVID J. LAKE

☐	THE RING OF TRUTH	UE1935—$2.95

NEW AMERICAN LIBRARY
P.O. Box 999, Bergenfield, New Jersey 07621

Please send me the DAW Books I have checked above. I am enclosing
$_____ (check or money order—no currency or C.O.D.'s).
Please include the list price plus $1.00 per order to cover handling
costs.

Name _____

Address _____

City _____ State _____ Zip Code _____

Please allow at least 4 weeks for delivery